Hon. Mrs. Fetherstonhaugh

Kingsdene

Vol. I

Hon. Mrs. Fetherstonhaugh

Kingsdene
Vol. I

ISBN/EAN: 9783337251765

Printed in Europe, USA, Canada, Australia, Japan

Cover: Foto ©Andreas Hilbeck / pixelio.de

More available books at **www.hansebooks.com**

KINGSDENE.

A Novel.

BY

HON. MRS. FETHERSTONHAUGH,

AUTHOR OF "KILCORRAN."

"Had no star ever appeared in the heavens, to man there would have been no heavens."—*De Quincey.*

IN TWO VOLUMES.

VOL. I.

LONDON:

RICHARD BENTLEY AND SON,

Publishers in Ordinary to Her Majesty the Queen.

1878.

CONTENTS OF VOL. I.

CHAPTER I.

STELLA.

" Sculptors of life are we as we stand
With our lives uncarved before us,
Waiting the time when at God's command
Our life-dream shall pass o'er us."

T is early on a bright June morning, and the little steamer *Electric*, from the north of Ireland to Liverpool, is slowly making her way up the Mersey towards the latter destination. In consequence of the quantity of shipping crowding the river, she is brought to a stop about once in every five minutes, and her weary and impatient passengers give utterance to many an audible moan and complaint.

1—2

One amongst their number, however, appears to take the unavoidable delay with stoical indifference, probably the result of his having already partaken of a cup of tea and a square foot of bread-and-butter, which renders him less clamorous for breakfast than his hungrier and more suffering brethren, whose constitutions have been somewhat shaken by the peculiar short roll of the little *Electric* when meeting the wind sideways off the Isle of Man at three a.m. that morning.

The said passenger is a tall, slight, fair young man of about five-and-twenty, who is leaning against the pile of luggage covered over with a tarpaulin, which encumbers the small steamer's deck, and listlessly observing the numerous vessels of every description and from every clime as they glide slowly past.

A sudden commotion on board causes all eyes to turn towards a large steamer which is passing the *Electric* on the starboard side, and Sir Gordon Leslie rouses himself sufficiently to take a pair of race-glasses out of his travelling-bag, and scan the faces of her passengers, as the Inman Royal Mail Steamer, *City of Montreal*, glides slowly and majestically past.

An uninteresting survey enough it proves, until a blaze of red-gold hair gleaming in the morning sun attracts his eye. But, " It's only a child after all !" he mutters discontentedly, as a second inspection convinces him of the latter fact, and any further discoveries are effectually put an end to by the indignant pitching and rolling of the little *Electric*, as she catches the " wash " of the larger steamer in full force.

Two hours later, after a careful toilette has somewhat restored his moral and physical equanimity, Sir Gordon Leslie makes his way into the coffee-room of the Adelphi Hotel, with a view to breakfast-ing before leaving Liverpool by the London express.

Only three of the tables are occupied : one by four or five men whose keen haggard faces seem to say that business and not pleasure is the motive-power in their lives ; another by a party of both sexes, whose accent betrays their New World nationality ; and the last by a very small figure clad in black, who is sitting in solitary silence and swinging one foot disconsolately, as she wistfully watches the gay, cheerful faces of the somewhat noisy party of Americans aforesaid.

A queer little, dark, impish face has this small specimen of womanhood, whose years can scarcely number more than eleven at most, and at the first glance little else is revealed than a shock of red-chestnut hair and a gleam of dark brown eyes.

Gordon Leslie asks for a morning paper, and is speedily buried in its columns—from the interest of which even the arrival of his breakfast can scarcely rouse him. Suddenly a light step comes alongside of his chair and a small brown hand is laid on his arm, whilst a childish voice says :

" Please, isn't this yours ?"

Sir Gordon looks up with a start, and smiles at the sight of the little sable-clad figure with its merry, mischievous *gamin* face, whilst, taking the smart blue silk note-case out of her proffered hand, he exclaims :

" A thousand thanks, little woman ! You've saved me no end of bother by finding that. Where was it ?"

" I found it lying on the floor out there by the window when I first came in, and so I waited a minute to see who it belonged to."

" And what made you guess that it was mine ?"

" Oh ! because a thing like that would only belong to a gentleman, not to people like those behind us." And a shrug of the small shoulders testifies to the speaker's contempt for the *bourgeois* element as represented by the other occupants of the coffee-room.

"Have you had breakfast?" inquires Sir Gordon, somewhat at a loss how to show his gratitude for the service just done him—which, as the smart blue note-case contains all his worldly wealth at this moment, is no trifling one.

"No, and I should like some very much," returns his new acquaintance without a shadow of hesitation.

"Well, then, sit down, and let's finish mine and order some more."

"May I really? and may I pour out the tea? I've done it often before."

"You shall do anything you like."

"This *is* nice!" exclaims the small

visitor towards the end of breakfast, and poising her last piece of muffin artistically upon three fingers ; " but aren't you afraid of what old Bloss 'll say to you when she comes ?"

" Who's old Bloss ?"

" Why, the fat old woman who took charge of me on the ship. She's coming in a few minutes to start me off for London. Her real name is Mrs. Major Blossom, but that's too long."

" Quite too long. I shall call her Bloss too when——"

" Young man !" and a stentorian voice from behind makes both of them start guiltily ; " I am truly grieved that this child, whose sinful tendency to forward-ness and undue exaltation of spirit has been the source of much tribulation to me throughout the voyage across the Atlantic, should have so far forgotten herself as to laugh and jest and eat with a stranger, as if he were her own brother! Were she my own child things would indeed be different!" and Mrs. Major Blossom sniffs with portentous meaning.

"But I ain't," retorts the small sinner referred to, "so don't worry me, there's a good woman, else I won't do your back hair for you before I go, and you know that your own arms won't reach to the back of your head, Bloss."

"Stella!" gasps the outraged matron.

"It's true," pursues the imp, encouraged by the visible laughter in Gordon Leslie's eyes. "You know that if ever you try so much as even to smooth your hair, all your strings and buttons fly directly, and it's just tempting Providence to do the little tail at the back."

" I cannot permit this impertinence !" and Mrs. Major Blossom advances firmly upon the small culprit before her, but is only confronted by a pair of little black legs, as the owner of the latter appendages goes to ground under the table with an agility which speaks of much previous practice.

" It is all my fault," says Sir Gordon apologetically to the exasperated lady. " I asked the little girl to have breakfast with me, so you must not scold her when I alone am to blame. She tells me that she has to go on to London by the next train ; perhaps you will let me be of use in taking charge of her to her journey's end ?"

Here a sudden convulsion of the table-cloth beside him reveals a momentary glimpse of a little dark, gipsy face, the grin of delight on which expresses full satisfaction at the impending arrangement; but it disappears again with pantomimic celerity.

"You're very good, sir. But I should not like to trouble a stranger so much."

"It's no trouble to me at all, I assure you. She did me a great service just now in returning something I had lost, and I should like to be of use to her in return. I believe it is quite time we started now, so will you tell her?"

But no orders are necessary on this occasion, for Miss Stella emerges slowly from beneath the table, smooths her hair, puts her hat down firmly on her head, and slides one hand into that of her new chaperon with a triumphant nod at her old one.

" Good-bye, Bloss," she says ; " I'm sure you're sorry to see the last of me !" and though the tone is one of bravado, there is a suspicious shake in the child's voice, and Sir Gordon feels her hand fidgeting nervously.

But the momentary trace of feeling fades speedily, as Mrs. Major Blossom gives her parting benediction with the severe austerity suitable to unreclaimed sinners, and Miss Stella walks out of the coffee-room humming the tune of the latest comic song, and spends the last moments of their uncongenial companion ship in an attentive study of the coloured flags painted over the sailing-lists of the different lines of Atlantic Mail Steamers, which decorate the entrance walls in the Adelphi Hotel.

When once the London express has got fairly under way, and is tearing along at forty miles an hour through the flat uninteresting bit of country surrounding our greatest commercial seaport, Sir Gordon makes a careful and minute survey of his new fellow-traveller.

Somewhere has he seen that wild, dark, impish face before. But where? for the life of him he cannot think, though it is an uncommon one enough. Its intense paleness is rendered more striking by the blackness of the eyebrows and of the long sweeping eyelashes which cover the mis- chievous, merry brown eyes, with their queer look of waggishness like those of a dog when he wants to play, and yet with all the faithful honesty of a dog's eyes in them too. A mass of tawny, red-gold hair completes the picturesqueness of the child's appearance, though a somewhat wide mouth and a nose with a most decided upward tendency at the point, rob her of all pretensions to real beauty.

She, on her side, is also quietly inspecting her *vis-à-vis*, and summing him up in her own mind. His frank, fair face, with its expression of perfect refinement, and his courteous friendly manner, have already made a great impression on her youthful imagination; and though to a more experienced observer the indolent, *insouciant* expression of the handsome face might tell its own tale of weakness of character in some points, still the firm, clean-cut mouth, which a slight brown moustache scarcely hides, and the strong square chin below it, vouch for strength of character being there should it ever be really called on.

Gordon Leslie's face was one of those that irresistibly made one doubt his power of choosing wisely in the great lotteries of life, and yet that made one also realise that whatever his choice might be, no power on earth could shake his adherence to it, whether it were for evil or for good.

CHAPTER II.

FELLOW-TRAVELLERS.

" ' What is life, father ?'
        " ' A battle, my child,
Where the strongest lance may fail,
Where the wariest eyes may be beguiled,
  And the stoutest heart may quail.
Where the foes are gathered on every hand,
  And rest not day or night,
And the feeble little ones must stand
  In the thickest of the fight.' "

                       Life and Death.

" YOUR name's Stella, isn't it?" inquires Sir Gordon, by way of a start.

"Yes. And yours is Sir Gordon Leslie. I saw it on your portmanteau just now."

"It's very odd, but I've been thinking for the last hour that I've seen your face before, and I've just remembered that it's in a picture which I've got at my rooms in town."

"What is the picture?"

"A little girl with hair just like yours, swinging in a hammock amongst the branches of a big tree. I bought it in New York when I was over there two years ago, and the picture was by a young artist called Claud Ray."

"He was my father, and the picture *was* me," says Stella quietly.

"Really? I am very glad. But what brings you over here by yourself, Stella?"

"He's dead," answers the child sorrowfully, "and so's mother. And a letter came out from England to say that I was to be sent over there directly, to an uncle and aunt who live in London, and Bloss was asked to take charge of me on the ship—that's all."

"What's the name of the uncle to whom you are going?"

" I forget, but it's written down here."
And a crumpled envelope is produced from
the child's pocket.

" G. Brabazon, Esq.,

E——n Square,

London, S. W.,"

is read out by Sir Gordon, followed by the
exclamation :

" Why he's a relation of mine too ! At
least, he married a cousin of mine, which
I suppose makes him one also."

" Oh ! then do tell me, are there any
other little boys or girls there, or anything
nice ?"

" There are no little girls there, I'm
afraid, and no little boys either. Both
Mr. Brabazon's daughters are grown up.
Which do you like best, boys or girls ?"

"Oh! boys, of course," responds Miss Stella unhesitatingly. "What are the Miss Brabazons like, please?"

"In what way do you mean?"

"Are they fine ladies and go to a great many parties, and do they prink and pretty themselves very much, and do *this?*" Here an artistic rub on each small cheek shows that the mysteries of the toilette are not an utterly unrevealed secret to Miss Stella Ray.

"Well, I hardly know," returns Sir Gordon hesitatingly, conscious in his own mind that the child has accidentally hit on an exact description of the Misses Amelia and Clara Brabazon. "But I dare say you'll like them very much."

"Oh no, I shan't. At least, I don't mean to if I can help it."

" But that's very silly of you if you
have got to live with them, Stella."

" Perhaps ;" and the child gives a careless shrug of her shoulders. " But not
one of them ever wrote a kind word
to mother when she was dying and
wanted it ever so, and I'll hate them
as long as I live !" she adds vehemently,
her eyes all ablaze with sudden excitement.

Sir Gordon wisely concludes that there
is more in this story than meets the eye,
and privately decides to inquire more
fully into its details the very first time
that he goes to see his relatives in E——n
Square. In the meantime he purchases
picture papers without end to amuse his
little companion, and by the time the
afternoon is nearly gone and they are

rapidly nearing their destination, both have become the best of friends.

Stella's quaint comments on all subjects in general, and her merry mischief with its slight dash of shrewd, unchildish sarcasm, amuse her companion immensely on the whole; and the picture of the struggling artist's home in New York, with its few short hours of joy and pleasure and its endless days of toil and pain, is painted vividly before him with all a child's un-hesitating candour and remembrance of small details.

That Claud Ray was an American artist who had married an English girl related to his (Sir Gordon's) own family, he can gather; but what the motive can be which induces his most astute and somewhat selfish cousin, Mr. Brabazon, to burden himself with the charge of a friendless little orphan like Stella, entirely passes his imagination.

He glances across at the child, who has laid her head wearily down on her folded hands as they rest on the cushioned ledge of the railway-carriage, and a feeling of sincere commiseration steals into his heart at the thought of this poor little wild mortal's fate, destined for the future to be caged in a cold uncongenial atmosphere of starched propriety, with never a friend of any sort to stand between her and the changes and chances of this mortal life.

"Stella," he says gently, "are you tired? I'll put this rug round you and then you could have half an hour's sleep before we get into London."

" No, thank you."

The tone is short, almost brusque, but
the child's eyes glisten like a dog's when
it has received an unexpected caress.

" At this moment you are in exactly
the same attitude as that in my picture of
you, Stella ; a picture which I shall value
far more now than I ever did before. And
strange to say, when I first saw you this
morning on the deck of the *City of
Montreal* as she passed our steamer, you
were leaning your head on your hands in
just the same way then too."

" It seems so odd that you should
have one of our pictures," says Stella
dreamily ; the one word " our " showing
how complete had been the mutual love
and sympathy between the artist and his.
little daughter.

" I'm very glad I have, any way. And I'll show it to you some day, if Mrs. Brabazon will let me take you out for a walk."

" Take me out? Oh! would you really?" And Stella's head is raised from its recumbent position with energetic abruptness. " I was just thinking that it would be so lonesome in London with everybody I hate ; but if I saw *you*, and went for a walk, I'd be having a good time at once !"

" Very well, you may count on that ' good time ' for certain then, Stella, if so small a thing can give you one. I wish I were your age, child !"

" Why ?"

" Because it would take a deal more than a walk or a picture to give me what you call a 'good time,' little woman."

"Then you've had it all good times, I expect," observes Stella gravely.

"There's a good deal in that, I dare say, Miss Philosophy! What a pretty name yours is, Stella; but I like the word 'Star' even better."

"So did father. He always called me Star."

"Then I shall say it sometimes too, Star, if you'll let me. The name seems to suit you somehow; to-day, when I first saw you, your hair made a bright spot on the deck of that great steamer just like a little morning star, and now in this. dull red sunset it lightens up like an evening one!" And Gordon Leslie looks kindly at the small downcast face of the forlorn little figure opposite him. "Here we are at the very end of our journey at last," he adds, as the train slackens its pace and wends its way through the masses of buildings and roofs of miserable, ill-ventilated houses crowded together on each side of the railway lines which intersect the great Metropolis. "Good-bye, Stella," he says, as the little girl rouses herself wearily and looks anxiously out of window as if to judge of the sort of appearance her future city of residence presents.

The rays of the setting sun light up her hair in a blaze of red gold, and the child looks almost beautiful as for once the usual "devil-may-care" expression on her face gives way to a softer one of honest loving gratitude as she says :

" You've given me a real good time
to-day, and I shan't care now what my
uncle and aunt and cousins are like.
Good-bye, Sir Gordon," and the small
pale face is held up to his to be kissed,
with all a child's frankness.

Gordon Leslie stoops and kisses her
with the words, " Remember, Stella, if
you ever want a friend you may always
trust in me ;" and then prepares to help
his little companion out on to the platform, and to find those of his relatives who
would no doubt have come to meet her.
But no one is there to represent the
Brabazon household except a tall footman,
who intimates that the carriage sent to
fetch " Miss Ray " is standing lower down
the platform, and politely offers to find
her luggage if necessary.

"One of my cousins might at least have come to meet you!" says Sir Gordon in a wrathful tone to Stella, as he takes her through the bustling crowd down to where Mr. Brabazon's carriage stands waiting.

"I don't care. I hate them!" answers the child defiantly; but by the sound of her voice he can tell that the coldness of her welcome in this strange land has gone, sadly home to her little heart, and a feeling of sincere compassion comes over him as he watches the carriage drive away, carrying with it the forlorn and friendless little mite which sits in a small black heap in one of its comfortable corners. But after so many long dull days at sea, the bustle and noise of the streets soon raise Miss Stella's spirits to their naturally high pitch, and by the time that the carriage draws up at her uncle's door and the tall footman announces her arrival by a loud and prolonged rat-tat-tat, the child is quite prepared to face any number of strange faces and hated relatives, and her face has assumed its usual mischievous *gamin* look; whilst not even the richness of the thick velvet-pile carpets under her little Bohemian foot, nor the splendour of the large rooms into which she is solemnly ushered, are able to awe her little soul in the very smallest degree.

CHAPTER III.

THE NEW HOME.

" Golden days—where are they ?
　Ask of childhood's years,
　Still untouched by sorrow,
　Still undimmed by tears :
　Ah, they seek a phantom future,
　Crowned with brighter, starry rays ;
　Where are they, then, where are they,
　　　　Golden days ?"

T is now ten days since little Stella Ray's arrival at her uncle's house, and she is sitting with the rest of the family at luncheon in the big dining-room at E——n Square, a meal which to herself at least means dinner. Nor does it seem much less also to the stout, handsome, elderly woman who sits at the head of the table with her back to the light, for she obviously carries out the truth of the saying that "luncheon is the ladies' meal." Neither does she forget to heap viands of every sort, wholesome or unwholesome, on the plate of the little sable-clad girl sitting beside her, and out of sheer gratitude for Mrs. Brabazon's well-meant though somewhat overpowering kindness, Stella Ray does her best to consume some portion at least of the delicacies showered upon her.

On considering the matter seriously, the latter young lady is obliged to own that, as far as perfect liberty and careless kindness go, she has little to complain of in her present place of abode; and if her heart aches from loneliness and want of companionship sometimes, and life in the small dull schoolroom upstairs seems lonely and sad enough, still there are many favourable facts to be set against the unfavourable ones, and, take it all in all, she is far happier than she ever expected to be in her London home.

The chief drawback to this happiness consists in the incessant snubbing she receives at all hours of the day from her eldest cousin, Miss Amelia, into whose disfavour she has unfortunately fallen through inadvertently alluding to some of the latter's "toilette mysteries" before an assembled circle of strangers. Her younger cousin Clara also, though of too apathetic a disposition to feel actively unkind towards any one, invariably followed her sister's lead by giving a feeble, lisping echo to Amelia's sarcasms.

Mr. Brabazon, Stella's uncle and now sole guardian, treated the little girl with fair kindness on the whole, though too selfish a man to trouble his head very much over anything so uninteresting as a child not yet in its teens, and his wife fairly overpowered the little girl with lavish kindness of the animal sort, *i.e.*, unbounded food, warmth, and clothes; but no ray of real womanly tenderness or kind motherly and sisterly love was ever offered to the little orphan cast among them in all her lonely desolation, and from first to last no thought of "home" was ever connected in Stella Ray's mind with the gorgeous house in E——n Square.

"Amelia, did you say that we could or could not get that box at Covent Garden to-night, my dear?" inquires Mrs. Brabazon in a tone of lazy interest.

"I really don't know, mamma," responds

Miss Brabazon, a look of vexation crossing her handsome face as she speaks. " We met Gordon Leslie in Bond Street this morning as Clara and I were coming back from Madame Pouff's, and he said he'd go everywhere to try and get us one."

" I like that boy," exclaims Mrs. Brabazon in her loud hearty voice. " He's good-natured, and he's a thorough gentleman, which is rare nowadays."

" What has he done to gain so much of your favour, mamma?" asks Amelia. " Evidently he has taken care to stroke your pet cat and yourself the right way and not the wrong," she adds sarcastically.

" Yeth, that he hath," lisps Clara in echo.

" He's done nothing in the world, my

dears, except to show me ordinary courtesy and civility on all occasions. But I am an old enough woman to know that it's not every young man of four-and-twenty who not only can but will remember to be civil to old bodies like myself. What do you think, Miss Stella, eh?"

" I think that Sir Gordon would," says Stella half shyly.

" How on earth do you know anything about him, child?" inquires Miss Brabazon in a contemptuous tone.

" Because he brought me all the way from Liverpool to London the other day, when I came here, and so I know that he's what Aunt Brabazon says."

" What did she say?" cross-questions Amelia teasingly.

" That he's a gentleman."

" There's nothing so extraordinary in that, you little monkey ! Isn't every one you see here a gentleman ?"

" No," says Stella, irate but determined, " that was a very mean man who dined here last night !"

" You little wretch ! what are you talking about ? Why do you call Sir Soapy Bland a mean man ?" exclaims Miss Amelia in tones of excitement.

" So he is a mean man ! I heard him promise that pug dog of his to Clara before you came down, and then when you went at him and asked for it, he jumped round right away and said you should have it."

" It's not true !" exclaims the outraged Amelia.

" It ith true that he did promithe it to

me firtht," lisps Clara tearfully. " And of courthe he'd have given it me if you hadn't gone and *athked* for it," she adds with an indignant whimper.

" He wanted to give it to me all along, only he was too shy," persists Amelia.

" That's a good one !" puts in Stella, on whom the florid countenance and saponaceous manners of the gentleman under discussion had made anything but a favourable impression.

" It wathn't kind of you, Amelia," murmurs Clara in plaintive monotone.

" Bless me, what a fuss over nothing !" answers Miss Brabazon. " Wait till the dog comes and then we'll see who he's meant for."

" He won't come at all," observes Stella with a grave nod of the head, but her eyes shining in mischievous glee as she speaks. "Because just as I passed that little sofa by the drawing-room door when Aunt Brabazon told me to go to bed last night, Sir Soapy was sitting on it with that pretty Miss Rosewarden who was dressed all in pink, and I heard what he said."

"What did he say?" exclaims Miss Brabazon with angry interest.

"That he had been obliged to promise his pug to the Brabazon girls for the sake of peace, but that he should tell them it had died suddenly, and that she, the pretty girl in pink, should have it this very morning," answers Stella, with a nod of her head at her two cousins, as much as to say, "There's one for you two."

"I don't believe it, and you're a very naughty little girl to listen to what other people are saying when it doesn't concern you," observes Miss Brabazon majestically.

" I didn't listen !" exclaims her small antagonist in hot indignation. " But he spoke quite loud, and I couldn't help hearing, any more than I could help hearing you tell Captain Euchrismer that you were going to take a walk alone in the Square Gardens this afternoon !"

The look of passive enjoyment on her sister's face at receipt of this last piece of intelligence greatly increased Miss Amelia's anger, and the thunder-cloud of her ill-temper was just about to vent itself in vials of wrath on her cousin's mischievous head, when Mrs. Brabazon— who had been calmly reading the *Morning Post* in utter oblivion of any passages of arms which it might please the members of her family to indulge in—suddenly exclaimed :

"Here's Gordon Leslie himself, my dears, so now we'll hear about our opera-box." And a ring at the door-bell confirms her intelligence at once.

The ill-tempered look fades from Miss Brabazon's face, whilst she smooths her hair and feels if her collar is sitting straight, with all the anxiety as to their appearance usually shown by the weaker sex when expecting the advent of the stronger. Even Clara rouses herself so far as to pull a chair up to the table for the looked-for visitor, taking care that it shall be placed in close proximity to her own, and altogether it is very evident that Sir Gordon Leslie is a relative who receives much favour from the Brabazon family.

He is welcomed as if he had just returned from the Arctic expedition, instead of a tour round the opera-box commissioners in Bond Street, and without waiting for the servants, Amelia helps him to whatever is hottest in the shape of luncheon still left on the table, whilst Clara goes through the unparalleled exertion of walking round the latter, to fetch the jug of claret for his especial benefit. She lost by this move, however, for Amelia took advantage of her temporary absence to make a pounce on her chair, which was next their cousin, a small piece of sisterly spite which Clara resented by a more energetic glance of contempt than one would have thought her vacant and unmeaning features were capable of.

"Well, Stella, how does life go with you?" asks Sir Gordon, pausing in the consumption of a *cotelette à la Réforme* to glance at the little dark face which is watching him with anxious interest from the farthest corner of the table.

"Very well, thank you, Sir Gordon," responds Stella cheerily, though a sad misgiving is coming over her that the promised walk with him to see her picture is a forgotten episode in his mind. Somehow this singularly good-looking young gentleman, whose faultless dress has long been a source of mingled admiration and jealousy to all his masculine friends, looks a very much less likely man to take a little girl out for a walk, than did the cheery, begrimed, and travel-stained young man in a rough shooting-coat, whose kindness on their journey to town had so won her heart.

"Well, but Gordon, my dear," interposes Mrs. Brabazon, "do tell us if you have secured a box for us to-night! The girls are wild to go and hear this new singer's *début*."

"Yes, I've got one all right, Mrs. Brabazon, but it was by a great fluke. All the world and his wife seem to want to do the same thing to-night, which is not only unfashionable, but extremely inconvenient."

" I suppothe it'th thith new singer that every one wanths to see," lisps Clara, with an engaging smile at her cousin. Unfortunately he is intent on scraping a small piece of butter off his coat-sleeve which he has had the misfortune to deposit there, so it is lost on him.

"Yes, it must be that, I should think ; but one hears very contradictory accounts of her."

"Tell us all you've heard," says Amelia gushingly, and rising to change her seat for one with its back to the light, having become conscious that the fact of " letting her angry passions rise " has imparted a more heightened colour to the tip of her nose than is desirable or becoming.

"I don't remember much, I'm afraid, Amelia," answers Sir Gordon. "She's a Mademoiselle Ida Stocker, a Norwegian, as you know, and is supposed to be extraordinarily good-looking, and to sing like a nightingale. She appeared in Paris last

4—2

winter and had a *succès fou* there, so they say."

" Is she very young ?" asks Amelia.

" No ; about three-and-twenty, I believe ;" which remark, though natural in a man of four-and-twenty, appears somewhat displeasing to the Misses Brabazon. " Villiers, in the Guards, is very much smitten with her, I hear ; and now I think I've told you all that I know about the young woman."

" You'll come and dine here and go with us to-night, Gordon, won't you ?" asks Mrs. Brabazon.

" Thank you very much, but I'm afraid I can't, Mrs. Brabazon. I've asked a man to dine with me at the W—— to-night."

" Well, but won't you come to our box

later, my dear boy ?   After all the trouble you've had in securing it for us you might just as well make it useful, you know ?"

" Oh yes, do,"—and " Pleathe do "— chorus the Brabazon maidens.

" Very well, Mrs. Brabazon, I will certainly manage it if I can," answers Sir Gordon, with no great show of alacrity, for, fond as he is of music, an evening spent with relatives crowded into an opera-box is not a prospect which holds out much temptation to him.   " I want to ask a favour of you now, Mrs. Brabazon," he continues, " and that is whether I may take Miss Stella out for a walk this after- noon ?"

" Take Stella out for a walk !" exclaims Amelia, as if she could not believe her own ears, and Clara's expressionless, light-

coloured eyes open wide in astonish-
ment.

"Yes, we're great friends, your little
cousin and I," answers Gordon Leslie,
nodding kindly at Stella, who sits awaiting the issue of this momentous crisis
with heart-felt anxiety. "And I've got
a picture in my rooms that I wanted to
show her, Mrs. Brabazon, if you'll let
me take charge of her for this afternoon ?"

"Of course you may, Gordon," responds
Mrs. Brabazon, in her usual tone of
careless kindness. "But must you go at
once ? Can't you come upstairs and talk
to us for a bit ?"

"Not now, I'm afraid. I've an ap-
pointment with a man at half-past three,
if Stella won't mind waiting in a shop

for half a minute while I speak to him."

"Then run along, Stella, and get dressed as quick as you can, my dear," says her aunt.

" And don't forget to see to that hole in your stocking which Clara and I spoke to you about this morning," calls out Miss Brabazon sarcastically.

" Thank you, Amelia, I'll change my stockings. But the hole wouldn't have shown in any case, for I went into your room this morning and blacked my heel with that stuff which you use when you're dressing for a ball, you know ;" and Miss Stella looks significantly at her cousin's beautifully and darkly-pencilled brows and eyelashes, and finally beats a retreat with flying colours, noting with delight, as she

closes the dining-room door, the super-
natural gravity of Sir Gordon's face, which
is quite sufficient to convince the imp that
he has thoroughly taken in her parting
shot into the enemy's quarters.

CHAPTER IV.

JE ME SOUVIENDRAI.

" Yet so it is with most of our lives. We play our parts without exactly knowing how or why. In the midst of all we deem duty, business, pleasure, we have rare intervals of tragedy and comedy, and these few moments fashion all our futures. Ten to one we never breathe a word about them. To our friends they are as if they were not ; to us they have been potent as life and death."—HENRY CURWEN.

"MRS. BRABAZON," begins Sir Gordon, the instant the door is closed, considerately turning his eyes from Amelia, who is vigorously fanning her flushed countenance; "I want you to tell me about this little girl, for if she's your niece she ought to be some sort of relation to me too, oughtn't she? Who is she, and what is she?"

"No, she's no relation to you, Gordon, because she is only my niece by marriage.

Who she is I can easily explain, for she's simply the daughter of Claud Ray, an artist and an American. He ran away with the only daughter of my eldest brother-in-law, William Brabazon, and though he never allowed them one penny, and they were in desperate poverty, I fancy the poor souls were happy enough in their way. William Brabazon never saw his daughter or her husband again, and they died last spring in New York within three months of each other. After that some artist friends of Claud Ray's took charge of the child temporarily, and wrote to her grandfather about her, which letter reached him on what proved to be his own death-bed. And at the last moment he altered his will and left that beautiful old place Kingsdene in W——shire, with five thousand a year attached, to this little granddaughter, and named my husband as her guardian till she should come of age, which she is to do at the age of nineteen, according to the terms of her grandfather's will. Of course we sent to America for her at once, and her friends in New York very kindly found her an excellent chaperon to travel over with " (here Gordon Leslie smiles to himself at the recollection of " Bloss "); "and now I've got masters for her and am doing my best to educate the child properly for her future position in life."

" So this insignificant little girl is owner of that beautiful old place Kingsdene," observes Sir Gordon musingly.

" Doesn't it seem too absurd?" comments Miss Brabazon severely.

" Certainly one can hardly imagine this mischievous, dark-faced little gipsy as the chatelaine of Kingsdene! But though she's got such a lot of devil in her, she'll make a charming woman some day, unless I am greatly mistaken."

"Well, I'm very glad some one sees anything to admire in her, for I don't," says Miss Amelia. "Such a hard-hearted, cheeky little monkey!"

" Meaning me, I suppose," calmly observes a small voice at the latter's elbow. " Well, good-bye, Amelia and Clara ; and don't keep Captain Euchrismer waiting," she adds in a confidential undertone to her eldest cousin, "for the Square Gardens are as hot as Pandemonium, and you know he can't afford to freckle much more."

"How I hate Amelia!" bursts out Stella, the instant that Sir Gordon and she are safely landed outside the house, and the hall-door has shut behind them with a bang. "Don't you?"

"No—o—o; not exactly," answers Gordon Leslie, with a great sacrifice of truth to prudence. "Don't you get on well with your cousins, Stella?" he adds inquiringly.

"Oh! we rub along. They snub me and I worry them; so it's all fair and turn about."

"But haven't you made friends with any one of them then?"

"No. Aunt Brabazon is very kind to me and I like *her*, but I hate the others. And there isn't so much as a dog in the house for me to talk to," continues Stella despairingly, "though I do coax the cook's cat to sit with me sometimes upstairs. But then she's only half a cat."

"Half a cat ?　I don't understand ?"

"I mean she can't purr, poor thing.　I may stroke her and stroke her ever so much, but she doesn't purr.　I suppose some of her works have gone wrong inside," says Stella dejectedly.

The interior economy of the domestic cat not having formed part of Sir Gordon Leslie's studies, he is unable to offer any solution to this unfortunate fact, so contents himself with an observation of good-natured pity :

"Poor little girl !　You must have a lonely life of it altogether ?"

"Yes, I feel badly at times," answers his companion in quaint, New World phraseology. "But I'm not going to think of it to-day, for I've got a long free afternoon, and no one to worry me," adds the child with a joyous laugh.

"Well then, we'll step out, and I'll just talk to this man I want to see on business for a moment, and then we'll go to my rooms and I'll show you your picture; and then we'll have tea, and I'll take you home by the Park, if you like, so that you can see the carriages."

"I don't care for carriages," answers Stella with the ungracious candour of childhood, "but I should like to see your home very much," she adds with all its genuine honesty also.

An hour later and the child is standing entranced before the often-discussed picture of herself, which occupies a prominent

place in the comfortable rooms in B——
Street, that are more of home to Sir
Gordon Leslie than is likely to be any
other spot on the face of the earth. For
though well enough off compared to many,
still he is no millionaire, nor is he owner
of any large landed estate; and as, in
addition to this, he has neither kith nor
kin belonging to him, there is nothing to
be wondered at in the fact of these
luxuriously - furnished   bachelor's rooms
being more homelike to him than they
could possibly be to those luckier ones in
the world, who have many abiding-places
and havens of rest in parent's, sister's, or
brother's houses.

The picture was a striking one enough,
but more so from the artistic grace of the
sketch than from the finish of the colour-

ing. The natural, weary abandon of the child's attitude as it lay in the reed-woven hammock, with its face laid on its small folded hands, and one bare rosy foot thrust out over the edge, was in itself a triumph of art; whilst the contrast of her tawny red-gold hair, with the deep bright green of the myrtle grove which made a background to the picture, gave to it a glorious dash of colour, and increased the picturesqueness of the whole effect.

It needed not the small and unpretending " C. R." in the corner to convince Stella then and there that the picture before her was no other than the identical sketch of herself done by her idolising young father when once, and for the only time in his sad, short life, he had taken a holiday with wife and child far away from the turmoil and clamour of the great city of New York, in search of that rest and peace which was only to come to him, after a long and weary waiting, through the portals of death itself.

"Do you remember the picture, Star?" asks Gordon Leslie in a low tone, half fearful of the deep wrapt look on the child's face.

"Yes," she answers quick and short; but there is a deeper meaning in this one monosyllable than in many a longer sentence.

"Come and sit in this comfortable chair by the open window and tell me all about New York, will you?" asks Sir Gordon, kindly trying to turn her attention from what was evidently still a painful reminiscence. "And then we'll have tea presently, and you must pour it out as you did for me at Liverpool the other morning—do you remember ?"

"Yes, that I do. And Bloss's rage too. Do you remember Bloss ?" asks Stella with her face all sunshine once more.

"Poor Bloss! you gave her rather a rough time of it during the voyage I expect, young person !"

"Sometimes I did," admits Miss Ray candidly.

"And how do you like your new lessons and masters, Stella ?"

"I don't like them, of course; but I know so little and I want to know so much, that I try not to mind them."

"That's wise of you," answers Sir Gordon, somewhat surprised at the serious tone in which his companion spoke. Evidently there was a deeper side to this mischievous *gamin* nature of hers.

" Why do you want to know so much, Stella ?" he continues.

" I thought it made people feel happier, perhaps," says the child wistfully.

" No ; you're wrong there, dear. The saying that ' knowledge comes with sorrow of heart ' is a very true one. Don't look so surprised, little woman ; I wasn't thinking exactly of the sort of knowledge which you mean, though."

" Oh !" says Stella, much relieved, but still more puzzled. " Didn't it make you much happier when you had learnt a great deal, and were grown up and knew everything ?"

" I'm afraid I never did learn a great

deal, Star," replies Sir Gordon, laughing. " And when I 'was grown up and knew everything,' as you put it, it most certainly didn't make me either a better or a happier man," he adds with some bitterness.

" Then I expect you learnt the wrong things," suggested Stella mildly.

" Perhaps so."

" Do you suppose that Amelia and Clara know a great deal ?" pursues Miss Ray, with whom this subject is evidently popular.

" I should think they knew a good deal for their age," answers Gordon Leslie, wondering in his heart what Belgravian daughters do *not* know !

" They chaff well, don't they ?" inquires Miss Ray with much interest.

"I don't know. Yes, I suppose they do. But, my dear Stella, to *chaff well* isn't the aim and object of a lady's education."

"I heard a lady say so yesterday afternoon to Amelia at five o'clock tea, and I asked Amelia afterwards, and she said this lady had travelled very much, and had had three husbands, so she must know a great deal, mustn't she?"

"Truly she must!" answers Sir Gordon in a tone of deep conviction; "but don't you try to copy the example of fools of women like that one, Star."

"I wish I knew who or what to copy," says the latter despairingly.

"Don't copy any one, child, if you take my advice. Go your own line, only see that it is a straight one, and try to keep as honest and true at heart as you can. There, that's all the advice I can give you, and I'm not sure that I ever offered even so much as that to any one else before."

" I won't forget," answers Stella resolutely, with a look in her brown eyes like that in a dog's which has been given something of its master's to guard and keep watch over.

" Here comes tea," says Sir Gordon, as his servant brings in a comfortable little table with its attendant tea-tray, and places it beside them in the window— showing that this was an habitual indulgence of his master's. " You pour it out, Stella, please."

" I dare say you never had tea poured out for you before ?" observes Miss Stella with confidence. " As you say you haven't got a mother or sisters ?"

" No, I haven't," answers her companion, wisely allowing one answer to stand for both questions.

" Shall you really go to the opera to-night, Sir Gordon, or were you only ' making believe ' when you said so to Aunt Brabazon ?"

" Which do you think, Stella ?" he asks, with inward amusement at the child's sharpness in having detected his prevarications.

" Well, I think you don't mean to go, for you looked as if you didn't."

" Do you think they all saw that too ?" inquires Sir Gordon, somewhat crestfallen. Like every gentleman of perfect manners, he prides himself on being able to " *mentir comme un dentiste*" (or, vulgarly speaking, to "lie like a black") with deserved success.

"Not they, bless you! They see nothing except what they want to see."

"I'm not sure that I shan't go after all, though," continues Gordon Leslie. "For its 'Faust' to-night, and not even the Brab—— I mean, nothing could spoil that." ·

"No; not even the Brabazons, I suppose," assents his companion with a mischievous chuckle.

"You won't tell them what I said, will you, Star?" begs Sir Gordon contritely.

"No, I think not. At least not unless Amelia is very knock-me-down. But I don't suppose I shall see her at all to-

night, and I dare say I shall have forgotten it by to-morrow morning."

"I hope so," remarks Sir Gordon fer-
vently, who feels by no means as certain
of this fact as he could wish. "But it's
time we were going now, Star, so get on
your hat and let's make a start."

As they near the door Stella Ray stops
short, and giving a look of regret at the
comfortable chairs and cosy tea-table by
the open window, she clasps her little thin
hands, and with a deep sigh of realised
happiness exclaims :

"I *have* had a good time this afternoon !"

"I'm glad of it, child," answers her
companion, almost touched by the tone of
deep gratitude in which she speaks.
"And if I were not going abroad in a

month or two for a very long time we'd have plenty more teas together."

"Are you going away?" asks Stella sorrowfully.

"Very soon I am."

"Oh dear! how badly I shall feel then!"

"No, you won't, little woman. Remember you are to work hard at all the new lessons, so that I shall find you quite a learned young lady when next we meet; and there are your riding lessons, too, don't forget. You won't have time to miss any one."

"Yes, I shall," answers Stella in a tone of sad conviction.

"Besides, it's the way of the world to forget," which is one more of the lessons you will learn some day, I fear, child!

But here we are at your own doorstep again, so good-bye, Stella."

" Good-bye, Sir Gordon, and thank you ever so much," says Stella, with a suspicious glistening in her honest young eyes as she slowly enters the Brabazon portals ; whilst her companion, courteously lifting his hat to her, strolls away with the satisfactory feeling of having anyway done a good-natured action, though he has spent his whole afternoon in the society of only a a child.

CHAPTER V.

" A NEW ' MARGUERITE.' "

" There lived a singer in France of old,
　　By the tideless, dolorous midland sea.
In a land of sand, and ruin, and gold,
　　There shone one woman, and none but she.
And finding life for her love's sake fail,
　　Being fain to see her, he bade set sail,
Touched land, and saw her as life grew cold,
　　And praised God, seeing ; and so died he."

Triumph of Time.

AR away under the pine-crested mountains of the Norse-land, stood the humble dwelling of painted wood which Hans Stocker had built for himself with his own hands many years ago, ere time had bent his form and furrowed his brow, or old age had weakened the sinews of his spare powerful frame.

A hardy old Norwegian was Hans, and the large family of tall, stalwart sons and lithe, handsome daughters which called him father, was one to make his aged heart beat proudly as he watched them toiling unweariedly through the burden and heat of a long summer's day, one and all intent on doing his or her share of the allotted work which was to bring prosperity and plenty to the humble home of the Stocker family.

Mother there was none, for she had died when her last baby was brought into the world, on the wildest, bitterest, Christmas Eve that could be remembered in all the country round for many years; but the eldest girl in the family had taken upon herself all the cares of the household, and had proved an honest, loving substitute for their lost mother to the little brothers and sisters depending on her. Now she was a careworn, elderly woman, whilst

they were still in the heyday of their
youth, but not one whit did she begrudge
the years of toil and trouble, and the long
life of self-sacrifice, which her care of them
had entailed upon her.

One summer's night, when all the rest
of the household were sleeping the sleep
which only comes to those who have
laboured hard and long from dawn to
sunset, Hans Stocker stood outside the
door of their home conversing earnestly
with his eldest daughter.

A strange incident had come to pass
that day, inasmuch as a stranger, who had
heard the glorious voice of Ida, the
youngest born of the family, singing an
old Norse legend as she followed the
cattle down from the mountains above,
had come and offered Hans red gold

6—2

down if he would allow him to take his daughter away and make a singer of her.

At first the old man had sternly declined to entertain the idea for a moment—"selling his daughter" he had called it with contemptuous brevity ; but slowly and surely the temptation which haunts men almost from their birth to their grave, the temptation of making money, had insidiously stolen its way into Hans' mind, and it was with an undefined feeling of impatience that he now stood listening to the anxious persuasions of his elder daughter to let the stranger go with a simple God speed, but to keep the little sister and daughter safe at home under her father's roof.

" The child is too beautiful to go

amongst strangers, father," murmured Christine anxiously.

" Not when she is a Stocker," answered the old man proudly. For peasants though they were, an unblemished name and an untarnished reputation, had been the portion of the Stockers from time immemorial.

" It is so far across the sea," continues Christine, "and she is so young to go out into the world all alone."

" Did not this stranger say he would bring his own wife up from the great town which lies beyond the mountains, herself to take charge of the girl ? Hast thou no pride, Christine ? What if thy sister were to become a great singer, and to sing before princes, and kings, and queens, would not that content thee, girl ?"

Christine shook her head sadly, and the weird brightness of the " northern lights " playing over her head seemed less unreal to her mind than did the dazzling hopes and prophecies which the old man laid before her.

He was too shrewd a judge of character to speak of gold or gain to any one of so single-minded a nature as Christine ; but in his heart he already saw the stranger's red gold laid out in numerous additions to his flock and herd, and who knew but what his daughter's voice might be the means of bringing wealth and comfort to him in his old age at last ?

So it was decreed that the beautiful youngest born Ida should be given over to the stranger's care, and should go to far-off foreign lands and become a singer there.   Christine's eyes were blinded with tears, when, for the last time, on one bright summer's morning, she braided the pale gold tresses of her fair young sister, and decked the heavy plait lying on each shoulder with a little bow of coloured ribbon, putting on her at the same time the simple green dress which had been her best for many a year.

Calmly, almost coldly, the young girl stood there, for the last time surrounded by those who had been her care-takers and play-fellows from her birth, and a pang shot through the heart of Christine whilst watching the careless indifference of the girl's look as she gave a farewell glance at the humble wooden dwelling which had been her birthplace, and at the rocks and streams and forest of fir-trees, that as yet had been all the world to her. Evidently she inherited her father's ambition and love for visionary day-dreams, for her last words to her weeping sister were :

" Comfort thee, Christine, and thou shalt yet hear of me as a great singer, and I will send gold enough home to make you all so rich, so rich !"

But Christine only covered her face and sobbed aloud at the loss of the fair young sister she would never see more.

Ida's prophecy came true, when after four years of hard study and unceasing application, she had made a triumphant *début* in one of our European capitals, and had sent back what seemed a small fortune to her old father in his far away Northern land. Old Hans chuckled as he carried home the bag of money from the big town beyond the mountains, which was only accessible when summer's heat had melted the snows that lay between it and the valley inhabited by the Stockers; and even Christine laughed and looked quite dazzled as the bright gold pieces were shaken out one by one before her eyes, for the winter had been a hard one and their straits had been sore.

"I wish the child had written me* one line only," murmured she to herself sadly. "Neighbour Peter's wife would have read it to me for sure. But I suppose she has forgotten, she was so young," said Christine pitifully.

It is six years now since Hans Stocker's daughter Ida had left her home to become a singer, and gone out into the wide world;

and after a most successful season during the winter months in Paris, she is now to face the ordeal of appearing before an English audience, the coldest and one of the most critical in the world, as " Marguerite," in Gounod's glorious masterpiece.

The crowded state of the house and its unusually brilliant appearance makes it very evident that some attraction out of the common is offered at Covent Garden to-night; and Sir Gordon Leslie has scarcely time to regret the last half of a pet cigar which he had heroically sacrificed in the fear of entering the Brabazons' box too late for Marguerite's first appearance on the stage, ere that event itself comes to pass.

When Mephistopheles shows Faust the vision of the maiden whose love he has promised him, and the form of Marguerite appears seated at her spinning-wheel in a pale, weird, shimmery light, a low murmur of applause sweeps over the entire house. Gloriously beautiful without doubt is the new Marguerite, and as the vision fades away, more than one there present would be ready to sympathise with Faust's reckless bargain of his own soul in exchange for the promised love of the beautiful peasant girl, Goethe's luckless heroine.

" Let's see her act, and hear her sing, before we decide on going into raptures over the fair Norwegian," said Sir Gordon critically.

But even he could find little fault with the fair-haired Marguerite as she sang the well-known " Jewel song " in her high, clear, silvery voice, that sounded like the bells of a mountain church heard far away amongst the hills. Nor could the most critical observer detect the slightest nervousness or want of harmony in the charming, natural grace of manner shown by the new actress in every gesture and movement of her evidently most carefully studied part; and as the curtain went down on the moonlit garden scene, and on Marguerite's answer to her lover's sere-nade, a thunder of applause shook the house from ceiling to floor, and time after time was the new singer brought before the curtain, bowing gracefully and coldly as ever to the excited audience which was giving her so enthusiastic a welcome.

" Yes, she's good-looking enough," assents Gordon Leslie, in answer to a remark from a friend of his, as both men stroll out of Mrs. Brabazon's box, to take a look at the house.

"Good-looking? is that all you can say, Leslie?" returns his companion hotly. "Why, the woman's positively lovely!"

"I dare say she is, my dear fellow," says Sir Gordon indifferently, "but she looks too much like an iceberg to suit my ideas; and I doubt her acting the finale to Faust's pretty little ramp half as well as she acted the beginning."

"Take care! here comes Dick Villiers, and he'll call you out if he hears you making disparaging remarks on the only woman he ever loved!"

"If Dick likes to make a fool of himself, that's no reason I should do the same," observes Sir Gordon carelessly. "He looks a bit in earnest though," he adds, as a tall, dark, gentlemanly-looking man hurries past them, with obvious inattention to every object save the one which is engrossing all his thoughts at that minute, and which, truth to tell, has been running riot in his brain for many a month past.

"Will he marry her, I wonder?" observes Gordon Leslie's companion in a tone of vague speculation.

"Hardly, I should hope. Though if Dick's monkey is up, there's no saying what he won't do. Come on, for they're turning down the gas with a view to the church scene."

The great expectations which the new singer's talent had raised in the minds of her hearers, were scarcely realised as the opera progressed. Though the inexpressible beauty of her voice was more than ever felt as Marguerite tries vainly to make her prayers to Heaven heard through the wild angry chorus of Mephistopheles and his demon satellites, there was a decided want of power in Mademoiselle Ida's rendering of the agonised, passionate despair of Faust's heart-broken victim.

True, each pose and gesture showed the actress's consummate skill in the reading of the part allotted to her, but the irresistible sway of real deep passionate feeling which carries all before it, was somehow wanting, and it was the actress, not the woman, who saved the conclusion of the opera from mediocrity. Still it was an undoubted success which this new Marguerite had won, and though Sir Gordon

Leslie put down his glasses with the careless criticism, " She's beautiful, but she can't *feel*," and though more formidable critics condemned the want of power and passion in her acting, Mademoiselle Ida's marvellous beauty and glorious voice held their own to the end; and long and loud were the calls before the curtain and the torrents of applause showered upon the fair Norwegian.

When off the stage, few would have recognised in the tall, graceful woman, with her cold, inanimate manner, the bright peasant girl whose voice had made the hills and valleys ring again in the old Norse-land. Still, as flushed with triumph she bent low before the tumultuous applause which greeted her, there was something in her plain, simple dress, and the heavy braids of pale gold hair hanging down on her shoulders which brought to mind the days of yore when she had only been "one of the people;" ere riches gained, ambition gratified, and success assured, had metamorphosed Hans Stocker's fair young daughter into the triumphant artiste and successful singer, whose fame all the world was conversant with; whose name alone made countless thousands throng to hear the voice which in days gone by had made poor Christine's heart ache with an unknown sadness whilst she listened to it singing some wild Norwegian legend as they sat spinning in the rays of the setting sun,—when she herself had still been a strong hearty woman and Ida only a bright fair child.

CHAPTER VI.

L'ISOLA BELLA.

"What though the pursuit may be fruitless and the hopes visionary? The result may be a real and substantial benefit, though of another kind; the vineyard may have been cultivated by digging in it for the treasure that is never to be found. . . . . . Many a generous sentiment, and many a virtuous resolution, have been called forth and matured by admiration of one, who may herself perhaps have been incapable of either. It matters not what the object is a man aspires to be worthy of, if he does but *believe* it to be excellent."—*Bacon's Essays.*

7—2

T is a hot sultry evening early in July, and though a deep-voiced old town-clock has just solemnly struck five, the heat of the sun as it blazes down on the little town of Domodossola in North Italy, is still powerful enough to make any exposure to its rays neither soothing to the body nor composing to the mind.

So thinks Sir Gordon Leslie as he stands in the shaded courtyard of the old-fashioned rambling "Hôtel della Città," peacefully smoking until such time as the atmosphere may have become cooler and fresher, so that he can take his walks abroad with the comfort which is inseparable from the true Briton's appreciation of the beautiful and the picturesque.

All the same he finds it rather a dull occupation on the whole, for, except two couriers laughing and chatting in one corner of the place, and an occasional glimpse of the dark-eyed daughter of the house as she flits along the wooden gallery running round the courtyard, there is not a living soul to be seen besides himself.

A great clatter of horses' feet and the rattle of a heavy carriage as it rolls in under the huge porte-cochère, acts the part of the Prince in the Sleeping

Beauty's history to the hotel in general. For out pour men, women, children, and dogs, of every description, intent upon attending to the wants of travellers, who, by arriving in a private carriage, have stamped themselves as " English Milords," and are to be robbed *ad libitum* accordingly.

" Why, how are you, Villiers ?" exclaims Sir Gordon, as he touches on the shoulder a tall, dark man, standing by the door of the carriage.

" Leslie, I'm so glad to see you, old fellow !" and Dick Villiers' tone is as hearty and genial as ever, though he is anxiously struggling with a perfect avalanche of fans, books, and parasols, which are poured into his arms by some one still inside the vehicle.

"Here, let me help you, Dick!" and Gordon Leslie makes an effectual raid upon the goods and chattels.

"Leslie, I forget if you have ever met my wife?" says Mr. Villiers inquiringly.

"No, I have not had that pleasure," answers Sir Gordon, who till this moment had almost forgotten the fact of his friend's marriage with the actress, Mademoiselle Ida Stocker, which had taken place a few months after her début in London, and now altogether about five years ago.

"Ida, this is Sir Gordon Leslie," says Mr. Villiers to the occupant of the carriage, and against the dark background of the same there appears what to Gordon Leslie seems the most beautiful face he has ever seen in his nine-and-twenty years of life.

A bright, fair face, with beautiful cold blue eyes that strike one like the touch of steel, a pink and white complexion, in which nature is so artistic and art so natural, that the most sarcastic critic must acknowledge what is done is done well, and a mouth, which, if it is a shade hard, has still much to boast of in the redness of the somewhat thin lips and the dazzling colour of the strong white teeth. The hair is fair and rather colourless, but contrasts well with the large black Rembrandt hat which covers Mrs. Villiers' head, and that her tall full figure is quite in keeping with her grand statuesque beauty is easily seen as she steps out of the carriage to greet her husband's friend with her usual nonchalant coldness of manner.

" Have you come here to-day, Leslie ?" inquires Dick Villiers.

" No, yesterday. And I mean to leave it the first thing to-morrow morning."

" Why ?"

" Because with the thermometer at ninety in the shade I can't be happy until I get to a lake or river, or somewhere where I can bathe, and they say the Lago Maggiore is only a drive from here."

" That's just where we are going to, so that'll be very jolly," observes Mr. Villiers, whilst his wife smiles in listless approval of his speech, but speaks no word.

" I wonder if any power on earth could

really wake that woman up to show a trace of feeling?" mutters Sir Gordon to himself.

Being young and extremely good-looking, he is generally accustomed to be met half way (or even more sometimes) by those of the fair sex whom he honours with his interest, and the perfect unconcern as to his movements vouchsafed by the beautiful Mrs. Villiers is somewhat galling to his *amour propre.*

"They don't give one a very good dinner here," he observes, reverting to the true-bred Englishman's just cause of complaint whenever slightly ruffled.

"Don't they? That's rather a bore, isn't it?" responds Mrs. Villiers in her slightly foreign accent, with a glance out of her blue eyes that renders Sir Gordon penitent in the extreme for his hasty judgment on her.

And as they turn and walk into the hotel, arrangements are made not only to dine together that evening, but also to travel in company next morning on their journey to Baveno, at which little town on the˙ Lago Maggiore the Villiers have decided to stay at least a fortnight.

A week of this fortnight had passed, before it dawned upon Sir Gordon Leslie that there are safer experiments in the world than trying to " wake up" (as he called it) even a cold and listless nature such as Ida Villiers', and a very unpleasant idea that whatever *she* might be, he himself was decidedly " waking up" in his interest for that lady, came slowly home to him.

Scarcely a day had gone by but that all three had taken themselves off together to spend what Sir Gordon called " a day in the open," which being interpreted meant that they paddled across the lake in a boat (which had previously been well stocked with provisions), and spent all the hot hours of the day sitting under the tall shady shrubs in the beautiful gardens on the Isola Bella, only returning to their hotel in the evening in time for a sort of late supper, after a good hard row about the lake had set the two men's consciences at rest in the matter of having taken sufficient exercise.

But this incessant companionship with the lovely Norwegian had proved a severe test to the invulnerable hardness of heart on which Gordon Leslie prided himself, chiefly upon the strength of having nearly reached the age of thirty without losing his heart more than was necessary or than was expected of him, and also having always regarded a *grande passion* with the contemptuous pity he considered such a weakness deserved.

Nor was the abject state of submission to which this last phase had reduced Dick Villiers, much of an inducement to him to follow in the latter's footsteps; and the first evening he had dined with the Villiers alone, it gave him a positive shock to see the meek way in which Mr. Villiers gave in to every caprice of his wife's, who apparently treated him much on the principle which is supposed to be the special right of the oppo- site sex: "something better than *her*

dog, a little dearer than *her* horse."
But as he grew more accustomed to
her manner, the supremacy of her marvellous beauty asserted itself, and soon
he would have preferred one only of
Ida's pale cold smiles to the sweetest
words that ever woman spoke or man
listened to.

"Where's Dick?" asks Sir Gordon,
glancing up at Ida Villiers' face as he
sits on a fallen marble column at her feet,
in the quietest corner of the grand old
gardens.

"I don't know," she answers, in a tone
which obviously shows that the sequel
to the sentence would be, "and don't
care!"

Ida's attitude as she leans back in her
low garden-chair is full of a careless grace

peculiarly her own; and that nonchalant indolence which is invariably assumed by a "daughter of the people" to hide the consciousness of past years, suits the passionless style of her beauty admirably. Her hands are very white, but large, and give one the idea that she could do real strong work with them an she listed (were not the bundles of pine-branches heavy, Ida, in the old Norse-land ?); but now their only employment is waving a large green fan sleepily to and fro, in the hope of giving artificial freshness to the air so heavily laden with the perfume of flowers and scented shrubs.

"It's horrible to think that we've only three more days to spend here," observes Sir Gordon sadly.

"Yes, I shall be sorry to leave this

place," answers Mrs. Villiers, favouring him with a glance out of her blue eyes which makes his pulses beat at the thought that it is the loss of his own society which she also possibly regrets a little.

" I've never been so happy in my life as during these last ten days," continues Gordon Leslie, " and if it were not for the thought of seeing you in London again during the winter, I should be ready to blow my brains out !" and the speaker's handsome face flushes with earnest-ness.

" What's the use of looking forward and building castles in the air, Sir Gordon ?" asks Ida coldly.

His face falls at her tone, but he re-covers himself and answers :

" I always look forward, Mrs. Villiers.

Châteaux en Espagne are so seldom really built that if one did not get at least the pleasure of anticipation out of them, everything would be Dead Sea apples altogether."

Ida shrugs her shoulders.

"I never build castles in the air," she says with a yawn of complacent laziness, "for I couldn't bear to see them fall."

"Few can, I should think, and one could scarcely blame them for it; it's a trial before which many have gone down, I expect," answers Gordon Leslie in a speculative tone. "But I'm too much of a gambler at heart not to build them up again and again, and always to think: they will stand this time."

"I believe I thought so too once, years

ago," says Mrs. Villiers dreamily. "And my castle really did stand that time. I mean when I became a singer."

This subject is one which Sir Gordon's intuitive tact teaches him not to enlarge upon too much to a woman like Ida Villiers, so he only remarks quietly:

"Yes, it was a brilliant castle enough, that of yours, Mrs. Villiers."

"And yet when it was built it gave me no real pleasure," answers Ida bitterly. "I liked the excitement of success, and the horror I have of poverty and all connected with it made me value my triumphs immensely from a pecuniary point of view; but I never felt the burning love of my art and the deep enthusiasm and excitement over it all, such as true artistes feel."

In spite of his infatuation for the speaker, Gordon Leslie cannot but recall his own criticism on her acting delivered long ago, and so makes no comment.

"I wish there were no such things as pain or hardships in life," continues Mrs. Villiers plaintively, holding up one large white hand as if to recall the memory of its earlier years of servitude. "I do so hate work and everything except sitting still and enjoying myself—don't you?"

"I'm afraid I've tried the former too seldom to be able to give any opinion, Mrs. Villiers; but I'll swear that a thoroughly idle life is much worse!" exclaims Sir Gordon.

Ida Villiers watches him with an amused smile as he raises himself slowly to take a good shot with a pebble at one of the dolphin's heads ornamenting the small fountain close to them. His hat is pushed carelessly on one side, showing to the full the fair handsome face of its wearer, stamped with the refined high-bred look which had been characteristic of the Leslies even in the days of the grand old soldier Sir David, the conqueror of Montrose at Philliphaugh, who received his spurs from the hand of Gustavus of Sweden himself on the field of Leipzig.

"You *look* so like a tiller of the soil," she says quietly and scornfully.

Sir Gordon does not hear the comment apparently, as he is engaged in pulling out and re-reading a letter received by post that morning, the first part of which he had perused in haste as it had reference to business matters of some importance, but the latter portion had been put by for a more convenient season.

The epistle is from Mrs. Brabazon, and he reads the conclusion carelessly :

" I feel quite grateful to my husband for desiring me to write this letter to you for him, as it gives me a chance of asking when we shall have you back again amongst us ? Also I must tell you a bit of home news : that Amelia is engaged to Sir Soapy Bland. Of course it is a very trying time for her, as the wedding is to take place soon, but she bears up wonderfully well on the whole."

("More than I could ; I should scrag the little beast !" mutters Sir Gordon in soliloquy.)

" You will hardly recognise Stella when you see her again, for she was at school during your last visits to us, and through all the London seasons, so I don't think you have seen her since she was quite a child. She's a charming girl, and in one more year will be of age and one of the richest heiresses in W——shire, so you might do worse, my dear Gordon, than make her Lady Leslie ; and this old place of hers is simply perfect. She's a clever girl too, and the way she has made up for lost time in point of education is simply marvellous ; but I can't make her care much for society, which is odd when one considers that a woman's province in life is to marry well. However she persists in preferring the country, and riding, gardening, or anything to the duties of society ; so I can only hope that time will show her the folly of trying to find a good husband, and above all a rich man, amongst the rose-trees and cabbages at Kingsdene.

"I must finish this letter now as Amelia and Clara are anxious to start for Lady Muffin's kettledrum, which is to take place at Crumpet Court, five miles away from here. It's a long, hot drive, I'm afraid, but the poor girls do so enjoy society, and in the country one must take what one can get.

"As usual, Stella laughs at the idea of what she calls 'social martyrdom,' and refuses to accompany us. She vexes me very much by these absurd ideas of hers, but I am sure that with a suitable husband she would soon amend her ways.

"Hoping to see you at home again before long,

"Believe me,

"Yours affectionately,

"MARY K. BRABAZON.

"KINGSDENE : *July* 13*th*."

"From whom may that long and apparently interesting letter be, Sir Gordon, if it's not impertinent to ask ?"

"Not in the least, Mrs. Villiers. It is from a most respectable matron with grown-up daughters."

"Then it can't be very interesting," remarks Ida listlessly.

"It is to me, for it's mostly written to recommend me a wife," observes Sir Gordon laughingly.

"I thought you had forsworn matrimony, Sir Gordon, but I suppose you have really only done so about as much as most men ; which means that they keep clear of it until *the* one woman turns up who has the power to make thorough fools of them."

"Don't you think I have come across my fate in that respect already, Mrs. Villiers ?" asks her companion, the laugh dying out of his face, and a wearied sad look crossing it. "Anyway, I don't think I'm likely to find my ideal in a little red-haired Yankee girl !"

"Is that a true portrait of your bride-elect ?" inquires Mrs. Villiers, with a cold, hard smile, which made one realise that she would be well pleased an it were so.

"It was when I last saw her, but I

hear she's a grown-up young lady now, and very pretty."

" Here comes Dick; I shall go and meet him," remarks Mrs. Villiers in a tone which, though the words sound natural enough, gives Sir Gordon plainly to understand that somehow or other he has contrived to say the wrong thing.

He racks his brains vainly to think what it can be, after the manner of fair-dealing honest young hearts which give " gold for silver " ungrudgingly, and yet so often have cause to bitterly regret the reckless expenditure.

So he follows his " daughter of the gods, divinely tall, and most divinely fair " with a slower step than common, as she saunters across the dried burnt grass to meet Dick Villiers, and also the lunch-basket; an existence on air alone being the very last stage of lunacy likely to find favour in Mrs. Villiers' eyes.

CHAPTER VII.

CHANGE UPON CHANGE.

" And my heart yearns baffled and blind, moved vainly
toward thee and moving,
As the refluent seaweed moves in the languid exube-
rant stream,
Fair as a rose is on earth, as a rose under water in
prison,
That stretches and swings to the slow passionate
pulse of the sea,
Closed up from the air and the sun, but alive, as a
ghost rearisen,
Pale as the love that revives as a ghost rearisen in
me."

Hesperia.

T is six years since we last saw
Stella Ray, and yet the slight
figure which is sitting close
before the fire that blazes in the big
drawing-room of Mr. Brabazon's house in
E——n Square on this dark November
evening, seems but slightly altered at the
first glance. The little dark face with its
honest, mischievous brown eyes is there
still; and though now the long heavy hair
is coiled neatly round Stella's head instead
of flying loose in the rough shock that

used to startle beholders of yore, it still possesses the deep red-golden tinge which is so rarely met with save in old pictures.

Though her figure is too slight to be really beautiful, there is little to find fault with in its lithe grace, born of natural activity and a free out-of-door life; but when the girl, starting at the sound of an opening door, turns her face towards the full light of the reading-lamp which is standing on the table beside her, few in the world would stay to criticise or condemn, when they are looking upon so brightly beautiful and lovable a little face as that of Stella Ray.

"Aren't you dressed yet?" inquires a harsh imperious voice, and Amelia Lady Bland sweeps up to the fire in a dress which seems to have an indescribable rustle and swagger in each one of its stiff folds.

"Yes, I'm ready for dinner," responds her cousin laconically, lifting her eyebrows in a critical manner especially annoying to her ladyship, as the full details of the latter's gorgeous robe unfold themselves before her gaze.

"Well, I think you might have taken the trouble to make yourself look a little nicer, I must say," continues Lady Bland with acerbity. "Especially as not only Gordon Leslie dines here to-night, but Sir Soapy also!"

A slight shrug of the shoulders at the conclusion of the latter sentence, testifies to Stella's contempt for the saponaceous Baronet whom she now has the blessed privilege of calling cousin. But she only answers lazily :

"Oh, I think I shall do, Amelia. You must remember I am not a bride with a trousseau waiting to be displayed, and no one will look at my humble white cashmere whilst they've got your magnificent toilette upon which to feast their eyes."

"Yes, I think this dress is handsome," murmurs the fair Amelia complacently, "at least, Sir Soapy says it suits my style to perfection, and he has such taste."

"No doubt."

"And whilst I think of it, Stella, Sir Soapy said the other day what a pity it was you didn't make more of your hair instead of twisting it so tight round the back of your head," continues Lady Bland, glancing sideways at her own chevelure in the mirror opposite ; and inserting a finger into one of its numerous puffs of hair, she gives it an affectionate tweak, unconsciously causing thereby an unfortunate interstice which reveals the frizzy foundation on which it is built.

" I'm very much obliged to Sir Soapy for the interest he takes in my head, Amelia, but I really can't wear frisettes to please him."

" Why not, I should like to know ?"

" Because I hate shams and humbugs of every sort and kind, especially wearing small bolsters made of dead people's hair."

" My dear Stella, how horribly you talk ! And even if it were true, that is no argument against it. If the fashion decrees that we are to wear our hair high, why we must wear it high of course, and if we have not enough hair of our own, it stands to reason that we must wear other people's."

"Do by all means if it pleases you, Amelia. I believe if the fashions returned to those of the Ancient Britons you'd wear no clothes at all, and only paint yourself sky-blue on state occasions!"

"Stella, you are becoming indecent. Sir Soapy observed the other day what a mistake it was for young girls to be so brusque in their manners."

"Toujours savon!" murmurs Stella irreverently, but before Lady Bland has time to vent her wrath in answer, the door is flung wide open to admit a tall fair young man, and Gordon Leslie's bright cheery face and kindly smile appear once more on the scene.

After enduring an effusive greeting from the fair Amelia, Sir Gordon turns to inspect the small figure standing quietly in the background behind her, and gives a positive start at sight of the change which time has wrought in his small playmate of years gone by.

" Truly the ugly duckling has turned into a swan," he thinks to himself, glancing at Stella's pure pale profile as it stands out clearly against the dark oak screen behind her, and the firelight plays on her red-gold hair and deep shining eyes.

" I should never have known you again, Star," he remarks wonderingly.

" Shouldn't you ?" answers the girl, with a bright sunny smile, for something in his tone makes it plain to her that the change seems for the better and not the worse in his eyes.

"Were you sorry to come back to England?" she asks shyly.

"I'm afraid I was rather," answers Gordon Leslie, reflecting on *who* he had left behind him in the sunny foreign lands.

"But it's quite right you should, you know," comments Amelia in a dictatorial tone. "I don't consider that young men of the present day perform half their duties towards society. It's nothing but sport, sport, morning, noon, and night; and when it's not that, it's a mania for staying in any country but their own."

"We're a bad lot, Amelia, there's no denying," responds Sir Gordon with a merry glance at Stella, who smiles back openly in answer.

"And the girls of the present day are every bit as bad," pursues her ladyship viciously. "There's Stella now, she'll garden or ride all day, or poke about amongst poultry and cottages everlastingly down at Kingsdene. But as to inducing her to devote her time properly to society, why it's simply impossible, though I tell her she'll regret it bitterly some day."

"How shall I regret it, Amelia?" inquires her cousin.

"Simply because you'll waste your best years in the life you're leading now, and it's not likely you will marry well if you continue to shut yourself up with only your dogs and horses down in W——shire."

"And is 'to marry well' the only goal of every woman's life, Amelia?" exclaims

Stella merrily. " I almost agree with you then that there's very little hope for me, as certainly the *jeunesse dorée* don't affect the solitudes of W——shire much until the hunting begins."

" Gordon, you've altered very little on the whole," observes Lady Bland, surveying him critically.

" Thank you, Amelia. Though whether you mean that for a compliment or the reverse, is not for man to say. Here comes your mother," and a warmer welcome than ever is bestowed on the guest who so invariably maintains his place of honour in Mrs. Brabazon's heart, spite of time and absence.

" Well, Gordon, dear boy, I *am* glad to see you back at last !" and both his hands are shaken heartily by his stout and cheery relative. " We began to think you were going to stay abroad for good this time. I can't even remember when it was you went away ?"

" Nine months ago, Mrs. Brabazon ; towards the end of last hunting season."

" Oh yes, so it was. Well, that sport will keep you safe in England for some time to come, won't it ?"

" Yes, I hope so. I've got the same lot of horses I had last year down at Leighton, and shall begin work at once."

" I thought you were going to give up hunting from town, Leslie ?" inquires Mr. Brabazon, whose arrival in the room has followed closely upon that of his wife.

" Well, I did think of it," answers Sir Gordon with slight hesitation, " but it will suit me better to stay in town this winter, so I shall leave things as they are." And he moves uneasily under the scrutiny of a certain pair of dark brown eyes which he feels are quietly watching him. "Stella, when will you come out for another walk ?" he continues, turning the conversation. "Do you remember our last one, when I took you to see your own picture?"

"Yes, I remember," answers Stella, and the merry wild eyes grow soft as a dream.

"We must have another one any day when Mrs. Brabazon can spare you," proceeds Sir Gordon.

"Oh, I can spare her well enough," observes the latter lady. "In fact, Stella very seldom condescends to come out with us when we go shopping or to pay a few morning calls."

"Then I shall feel especially favoured

if she will go out with me," answers Sir Gordon kindly ; but careless courtesy is obviously the mainspring of the remark, and Stella feels somehow a shade disappointed at the coldness of his tone.

"Gordon, you're not in as good spirits as you used to be," observed Mrs. Brabazon about an hour or so later, when the servants had left the dining-room, and the family party were once more left to themselves.

"I'm older now, Mrs. Brabazon," answered Sir Gordon, with a start which showed plainly that his thoughts had been very far afield at the moment. "Old age carries care on its crupper, and I am nearly thirty."

"That's not old enough to steady most men," remarked his hostess, "unless a man has lost his health or his heart."

" Let us hope it is neither of those losses which is affecting me," answered Gordon Leslie, laughing uneasily.

" Aunt, I heard a great smash of china in the drawing-room a minute ago," interrupted Stella Ray. And Sir Gordon, as he glanced at her, instinctively felt that his former little friend was making a diversion in the conversation for his sake. " I hope the new footman hasn't dropped the lamp which is always carried up about now."

" My dear child, if it should be that, I really don't know what I should do !" exclaimed Mrs. Brabazon in loud distress. " Let us come up to the drawing-room at once and see."

Sir Gordon held the dining-room door open for the ladies to go out, and again glanced at Stella's face as she passed him by. But the brown eyes were bent downwards, and not a trace of any unusual feeling was to be discerned on Miss Ray's countenance, though the instant that the dining-room door was closed between them a grave, puzzled look crept into the said brown eyes, and the laughing mouth fell slightly.

" There's something wrong with him, I can see that too," she thought to herself sadly ; " and I wonder who the woman is, and whether she's worth caring for ?"____

. Somehow this speculation, though no doubt interesting, scarcely appeared to be pleasing to Miss Ray, for the darkly-pencilled eyebrows met in a vindictive frown, and the high-heeled shoe came down on the top stair with a vicious little stamp.

"My dear Stella, how you have frightened me for nothing!" exclaimed her aunt, after a careful survey of the gorgeous drawing-room had convinced that lady that no damage had been done to her pet lamps, old china, or any other nick-nacks.

"I'm very sorry, aunt, but I spoke to save worse harm being done possibly," returned Miss Ray with a mischievous laugh.

"Well, all's well that ends well," observed Mrs. Brabazon good-humouredly. "Amelia, don't you think that Gordon Leslie is altered somehow?"

"Not in face. But he isn't half the fun

he was, and looks as if he were years older since we last saw him."

" Perhapth mamma ith right, that he 'th in love,"' lisped Clara, who since her soul had found its affinity in that of a junior clerk in the Foreign Office, was apt to jump to the conclusion that all other men and women were even as herself.

" You're always thinking of that nonsense, Clara !" retorted her sister sarcastically.

She had never wasted much thought on it, to do her justice !

Stella Ray said nothing, but the grave, speculative look remained in her eyes for the rest of the evening, and Sir Soapy Bland confidentially informed the wife of his bosom during their journey home, that her cousin was growing more airified and eccentric every day, and for his part he pitied the man who married her, even with all Kingsdene at her back.

CHAPTER VIII.

MERCI, FORTUNE.

"But, wherever this nature of mine is most fair,
  And its thoughts are the purest—belov'd, thou art there!
  And whatever is noblest in aught that I do,
  Is done to exalt and to worship thee too.
  The world gave thee not to me, no! and the world
  Cannot take thee away from me now.   I have furl'd
  The wings of my spirit about thy bright head ;
  At thy feet are my soul's immortalities spread.
  Thou mightest have been to me much.   Thou art more.
  And in silence I worship, in darkness adore."
                                      Lucile.

"I SEE by this evening's paper that poor Dick Villiers is dead," is the careless comment which falls on Gordon Leslie's ear as, an hour later, he enters the Surf Club.

"Wonder what that handsome wife of his will do now, and who'll have the honour of being her second husband?"

"Don't care, as long as it's not myself," observes the cheery young Guardsman who had first spoken; whereupon a discreet nudge from his companion draws

10—2

attention to the near vicinity of Sir Gordon Leslie, and an awkward silence falls on both.

"That's the man who'll marry her," murmurs the young Guardsman *sotto voce,* "and I'm sorry for it, for he's a thundering good fellow, and she——" an expressive shrug of the shoulders completes the sentence.

Meantime Gordon Leslie lights his cigar and sits down before the almost deserted fire as if in a dream. Slowly he realises in full force the meaning of the words he has just heard, and mechanically he takes up the nearest evening paper to read the news for himself.

There is no doubt of its truth, for the short, concise announcement of Mr. Villiers' death in Italy, through Roman

fever, is contained in the first paragraph
which catches his eye. He reads it
through twice, three times; and tries hard
not to rejoice even though Ida is now
free. He had been a good fellow, poor
old Dick, and a kind husband to *her*, God
rest him! But still all that was over
now, and no doubt he was better off;
whilst here stood his successor ready to
step into his shoes.

Try as he may, Gordon Leslie cannot
wholly repress a feeling of savage exulta-
tion over the dead man, at the thought
that the treasure possessed by one, coveted
by the other, and so passionately valued
by both, would now some day be his and
his alone. No doubt of Ida Villiers' con-
stancy crosses his mind even for an instant,
and, as he walks home through the silent

streets, visions of home and happiness, in which a glorious fair face appears ever pre-eminent, shine out before him and turn the dark and cheerless night into bright and dazzling day.

" My darling !" he murmurs tenderly, as, once more in his own rooms, he buries himself in a big arm-chair to think it all out. " I must give her a year, or ought it to be eighteen months ? No! I think a year is enough, and then I shall go and ask her to be my wife." And a smile of ineffable content crosses Gordon Leslie's face as he pictures to himself what Ida's answer will be. (Truly Balzac was right when he wrote : " Quand on aime, tout arrive à l'amour.")

" We'll go to Norway for our honey-moon, and go and see all her own people if she cares to," pursues the visionary in his thoughts. " I dare say they're a bit rough, but what does that matter? it won't make Ida one shade lower in my estimation to know that Burke never heard of her ancestors. Good thing on the whole, for then she'll be solely mine and will belong to no one else on earth of any sort or kind. Poor girl! I wish I could be with her now, but I suppose Mrs. Grundy would forbid that. Besides, I don't want to seem to rejoice over that poor fellow in his grave out yonder, before even a year is out. No, I shall hunt this winter, and then go abroad till Christmas, and after that—the deluge!

" My beautiful darling, what will you do and say when I come to beg for my life's happiness? It's maddening to think that more than a year must pass before I dare see you again except by chance. But I can trust you, dear one, and would wait till life's end, if need be, to receive even one word of love from you at last !"—

Oh, Gordon Leslie ! will nothing teach you that an honest loyal heart such as yours can never know bliss on earth ? That as long as life lasts it will wait and hope, bearing pain ungrudgingly and beating itself day after day against the bars in vain hope of deliverance and happiness to come, only to fall down at last, beaten and bruised and wearied in the strife ? It is the hearts of tougher though not truer metal than yours that conquer in this world ! who love "as much as they are able," taking care never to expend one grain of their store without a due and

satisfactory return, | and who carelessly
accept the greatest and goodliest love " of
man and woman when they love their
best, closest and sweetest," as a just tribute
and simple right.   Woe to these, if, when
the play is played out, the curtain dropped,
and life ended, they are called to account
for the faithful loving hearts which were
all their own.

On the afternoon of the next day two
people are walking briskly up and down
under one of the avenues of limes in
Kensington Gardens.

   "I thought last night that you were a
great deal altered, Sir Gordon," says Stella
Ray shyly, "but you're just what I remember you after all."

   "I heard some good news last night,

little woman, and feel as if the whole world had turned upside down for my especial benefit," and the speaker laughs out in his gladness.

" Anything I may know ?"

" Some day, but not now. Stella, people say a thing is 'just like a novel' when it's totally incredible, and yet everyday events beat any book that ever was written for utter improbability."

" I suppose they do," assents his companion with ready sympathy, though totally at a loss to know what he can be referring to. "But I often wonder why, when people are writing a novel, they must put so many unnecessary impediments in the way of their hero and heroine's ultimate happiness. The thread of their stories goes up and down and is lost and found, just like the original air in a piece of music with 'variations.' Why can't the good people run plump into each other's arms round a corner, and settle it?"

"I wish they could, in real life as well as in books," answers Sir Gordon, laughing. "But, Stella, tell me about Kingsdene, and all your people and animals, will you? Remember, I have never seen it; won't you ask me to stay with you some day?"

"Oh, I should so like it!" exclaims she, her face colouring rosy red with earnestness as she stops and looks into his face, the better to judge of the sincerity of his words. "Would you really come?" she continues with a sort of shy grace. "There's fishing and hunting there to amuse you, you know."

"Of course I shall come whenever you like to ask me, and the sooner the better. For when once you are married you will have all your husband's friends to entertain and will have less room for your own."

"I doubt if I shall ever marry, Sir Gordon. I don't say it as most young ladies do, because it sounds well, when all the same they intend to marry the very first man that asks them; but you see I have plenty of work cut out for me already, and even if I am an old maid I shall not have to lead a useless life."

"But granted that you have unlimited occupation and interest in your own life, even that can never be weighed in the same scale as home happiness and others to love and care for." And Gordon Leslie's

thoughts fly back to his day-dreams in-
voluntarily.

A vague, dreamy look sweeps over
Stella Ray's downcast face, as if she too
had dreamt of what life and love could
bring to her; but the love which could
make her reckless little heart bow before
it would have to be indeed a great one,
and a minute later her merry laugh rings
out as gaily as before.

" No, verily, Sir Gordon. No matrimony
for me, if you please. I don't know which
is worst : to be as rich as Crœsus as
Amelia is, with neither chick nor child to
waste her money on, or to be as poor as
Clara will be, and to subsist on love in a
cottage and the pay of a clerk in the
Foreign Office."

" But all the world isn't divided into

couples as rich and lonely as the Blands, and others whose only resources consist of an overwhelming supply of olive-branches. It's all nonsense for a woman to talk of living alone situated as you are, and the sooner you turn your attention to finding a young man worthy of yourself and Kingsdene, the better."

"Very well, Sir Gordon. Shall I begin to look out at once? Or don't you think I might commence my hunt on Monday? That's a very nice day to start on. They always hang a man on a Monday, I suppose that he may begin the week well."

"You may laugh, but it's the best of advice that I'm giving you all the same. Tell me, what do you do with your time all day down at Kingsdene?"

"Oh, there's plenty to do always. First

there are the gardens to look after, and
the farm and poultry, and the old women;
and then you know I've got two or three
horses," adds the girl hesitatingly, divided
in mind between an intense desire to tell
him all about her home life and the things
of most interest to her, and a dread lest he
should think she was taking too much of
the airs of proprietorship on herself.

"What are the horses?"

"Well, one is a brougham horse, because
you see Aunt Brabazon is there always
with me too, and she can't walk much;
and one is a sort of hack and light harness
horse which I ride in the summer, and the
third is my own particular beast, a hunter."

"I hear you can ride above a bit now,
Stella; is that true?"

"It's true if I'm on old 'Kildare,' but I

don't know if I should get on as well on other horses."

" Well, I hope to see for myself some day, if this anticipated visit of mine to Kingsdene ever comes off."

" But you've said you'll come," and Stella's brown eyes look into those of her companion with perfect trust and confidence.

" And I shall be only too glad to keep my word. But the event certainly can't come off this winter, and next spring I shall go abroad again for nearly a year."

" Shall you ? What makes you take these restless wandering fits so often, Sir Gordon ?"

" I took to them first from idleness, then because I wanted to forget, and now because I want] to remember. There, that's not a very intelligible explanation I know, Star, but some day I will tell you everything if you care to hear it."

"Yes, I shall always care to hear it, Sir Gordon," answers the girl quietly, then adds in a lighter tone : "look at this dear little collie puppy being led along ; I expect that man has stolen it."

It certainly was a beautiful puppy of its kind, and seeing the favourable impression made on the young lady, the ill-favoured, unkempt individual in charge of it stopped at once to offer it for sale.

"It's not a bad-looking puppy by any means," says Sir Gordon in a low aside.

"Poor little beast ! it looks so hungry," answers Stella pitifully, as the puppy looks wistfully at her and tries to find a forgotten crumb in the folds of her dress.

"Well, I don't mind buying it if you'll undertake to keep it, Star. I'm sorry for the poor little beast, but can't be bothered with another dog myself. But I'll gladly get it if you'll take possession of it and give it a home."

"Do you mean you'll give it to me?" exclaims Stella delightedly. "I should like that better than anything, for I'd value it for your sake as well as its own," she adds frankly.

"That's settled then"—and in another five minutes the collie puppy is following his new mistress with a contentedness of mind which does not say much for the treatment he has received at the hands of the unshaven and unshorn individual aforesaid.

CHAPTER IX.

BONS CAMARADES.

"Dans l'amitié et dans l'amour on est souvent plus heureux par les choses qu'on ignore que par celles que l'on sait."—Rochefoucauld.

INTER is over at last, though it has dragged its slow length far into the months which are sup-posed to be the sole property of its sunny-hearted sister Spring; and the first warm bright May day is this when Sir Gordon Leslie and Stella Ray are once more walking up and down under the lime-trees in Kensington Gardens, for the last time for many months.

These two have become firm friends during the winter, though Gordon Leslie

had after all spent almost every week of it
in the country hunting; still most Sundays
saw him at luncheon in E——n Square,
and then, as both the master and mistress
of the house invariably composed themselves after that meal for their Sabbath
afternoon's siesta, Stella and Sir Gordon
used to take advantage of the fact to
escape out of the house for a long *tête-à-*
téte walk, during which subjects of interest
to the world at large and themselves in
particular were fully discussed.

So it came to pass at last that the girl's
heart learnt the old, old story, whilst the
man went on his way scatheless and free.
Not that he didn't sincerely love the
honest little friend, who was always so
glad to see him and to give him her ready
sympathy whenever wanted (did she under-

stand the reason for which it was de-manded, or not); and no trouble could be too great for him to take to give her pleasure, or to help her in any way that was in his power. But the deep, unwavering nature of the man kept him true to the one great love of his life, and no other woman—let her be who she might—could ever have gained one shadow of influence over Gordon Leslie's true and loyal heart.

"It's very nice of you, Stella, to take my departure to heart," he says, in the gay frank tones which speak for them-selves in their utter carelessness.

"Is it?" answers the girl sadly. "I can't see that there's anything extra 'nice' in being sorry to lose one's only friend."

"But you have others already, and

somehow I don't think you're a very likely young woman ever to want for friends."

"I mayn't want for them, but I may want them all the same," says Stella quietly. "No, besides yourself, I have but one real friend in the world, and that is 'Collie' here," and the girl stoops down to lay her hand on a black-and-tan head which is rubbed lovingly against her at the sound of its own name.

"Collie" is rapidly developing into a discreet and sober-minded dog, not lightly led away; though at times his canine ideas of waggishness prompt him to indulge in sundry unexpected gambols of an alarming nature to the uninitiated; such as advancing across a room with ears cocked and in short, quick bounds of apparent evil intent, or sudden pounces on unwary toes under the table. But the honest lovingkindness in the expression of his tan, foxy face, and in his brown eyes, disarms all objection to any mischief on the part of so thoroughly good-hearted a young dog; and "Collie's" engaging manners have gained him a well-deserved popularity with both high and low.

"Who knows but what by the time I return you will have found your affinity in some W——shire landowner, Star!" observes Sir Gordon. "Why, I declare you're blushing. Has he turned up already then, Miss Stella, and have you been hiding it from me all this time?" and Gordon Leslie takes his companion laughingly by the shoulders and wheels her round so as to bring her hot crimson cheeks face to face with him.

"Let me go. Please let me go, Gordon. I'm really not blushing a bit," and Stella lays her little gloved hands on each fiery cheek in defiance.

"Then I can only say that your ordinary complexion is the same as that of a turkey-cock suffering from scarlet fever! Never mind that, though; it's not the fact of your being such a colour that I wish to inquire into, but what *caused* you to be so."

"I don't think there's any reason," begins Miss Ray hesitatingly; "at least not much of a one."

"All the same I should like to know it. And if it's a tender subject at all, I'll give in so far as to turn you with your back to me instead of your face, whilst you make your confession."

"No, you needn't;" and a pair of mischievous brown eyes meet his merry grey ones calmly. "I'll tell you what made me blush (if I did blush), and that is sheer rage. I've been awfully insulted lately, quite dreadfully, by a man having told Aunt Brabazon that he wished to marry me, and as he really is a W——shire landowner the cap rather fitted, do you see?"

"May I know who it was?" asks Gordon Leslie curiously, trying to comprehend and take in the astounding fact that this little playmate of his is a grown-up young woman whom men covet for a wife. Somehow, though he has often chaffed and laughed with her on the subject, the idea of Stella Ray belonging to another has never been realised in his mind, and a strong feeling of at least regret steals into it as he remembers how often her affection and sympathy have brightened the past to him. —

"It began the end of last summer," answers the girl, "when we were staying a month or two at Kingsdene. He was always coming over then, but Aunt Brabazon saw most of him because I wouldn't. I did hate him so, with his cold sneer, and his scarcely concealed contempt for every one except himself. Gordon, I always felt as if a snake were in the room when that terrible old man came into it!"

"*Old* man!" echoes Sir Gordon in surprise.

"Yes, it's old Lord Cunninghame I

mean; he lives at Winncote Park, quite near to Kingsdene, you know."

"Good heavens alive! Mrs. Brabazon would never think of wishing you to marry that old—sinner!" exclaims Gordon Leslie, correcting just in time a more forcible conclusion to his sentence.

"Indeed she would. He ranks high in 'society,' you see," remarks Stella bitterly.

Her companion looks unwontedly grave as he paces slowly along beside her. The character Lord Cunninghame bears, though high enough as regards the ordinary standard of social requirements, is not one to make any man rejoice at the prospect of his daughter, sister, or friend being consigned to the old man's tender mercies as his wife. And Sir Gordon

Leslie with difficulty represses a torrent of expletives levelled at the head of the hoary libertine old peer, which would have profoundly astonished that most polished and courteous-mannered of sinners.

"Stella, you must promise me, dear, never to think of marrying Lord Cunninghame," he says gravely. "I'm not strait-laced, God knows, but I'd sooner see any one I cared for dead than married to a man like that!"

"You needn't fear, Gordon. No power on earth should induce me even to think of such a thing."

"I remember giving you good advice once before, little girl, many years ago; and you took it so kindly then that I feel emboldened to offer it again now. Not but what I dare say you've totally forgotten the occasion I speak of and my words of wisdom then."

"No," answers his companion quietly. "You said: 'Go your own line, only see that it is a straight one, and try to keep as honest and true at heart as you can.'"

"You remember it better than I do myself, Star," and Gordon Leslie glances keenly at her downcast face, as for the first time a dim suspicion crosses his mind that his quondam plaything has grown into a living, loving woman.

"And I *shall* remember it," responds the girl briefly, but in a strangely earnest tone. "Now, having decisively settled Lord Cunninghame's merits and the exact amount of appreciation they deserve," she adds with a gay laugh, "let me hear something about your prospects, Gordon? Has not the mythical heiress, whom all men seem to go in quest of like a modern Holy Grail, appeared before your eyes yet?"

The instant that the random words are out of her mouth Miss Ray bites her lips and flushes scarlet with vexation. Is not she herself an heiress? And would not many men see a deeper meaning in her careless speech than had ever been meant?

But Gordon Leslie is too thorough a gentleman not to take her words *au pied de la lettre* simply, and he only answers dreamily:

" I don't think that marrying for money would ever be much in my line, Star; I'm too thin-skinned for it. If my wife possessed the mines of Golconda themselves and yet 'clashed' with my ideal, I should simply hate her. No! I have my ideal, as I suppose all men have, and it shall be *mine* in very truth some day, or man is more powerless against fate than I suppose !" and Sir Gordon's fair young face flushes with earnestness as he speaks, and his eyes kindle with " the light of other days," as the memory of a soft white hand and a bright cold smile set his heart beating as of yore.

Stella glances at him observantly, noting the warm, *living* look which has so suddenly crept over his gay *insouciant* face, and with unerring perception comes at once to the conclusion that nothing but a woman could have caused so great a change. Her heart feels sadder and heavier somehow than it did a few minutes ago, but she only asks in a tone of utter unconcern :

"Quelle est la femme, Gordon? I've told you all about my little idyl, mayn't I hear the tale of yours?"

"There's none to tell," answers Sir Gordon shortly, for his companion's tone of merry badinage accords ill with the chivalrous and loyal devotion which he feels towards the memory of his absent love; "and you don't care enough about me to take much interest in my story, so why should I bore you with it?" he adds, with all the injustice of a man when talking *to* the woman who loves him, and *of* the woman whom he loves!

Miss Ray's white teeth leave their mark on her little red underlip, but she only answers:

"Very well. Don't tell me anything, Gordon. I'm accustomed to expending my feeble sympathies on your behalf without having the faintest idea of the why or wherefore, so it's nothing new ;" but the speaker's voice sounds forced, and even Sir Gordon is roused from his memories at the sound of the almost weary tone.

" Dear little girl, I didn't mean to vex you," he exclaims with contrition. " Only you see when one cares very much indeed about any one, it's not easy to speak of them as if it was just an ordinary every-day subject, and so——" The sentence is brought to an abrupt conclusion as both Sir Gordon and Stella spring hastily back to avoid being knocked over by a neat brougham, which is being driven rapidly past Albert Gate just as they are crossing over the road on their homeward way.

Some one dressed in deep mourning is

sitting within the carriage, and a fair cold face leans forward to bow to Sir Gordon Leslie as he raises his hat with a bright sudden look of gladness that speaks volumes to the quick perceptions of the girl standing beside him.

"So *that* is his ideal," she thinks to herself sadly, as with all a woman's acuteness in noting small details, she realises that a more perfect contrast to herself than the said "ideal" apparently exhibits could scarce be found in all the length and breadth of England.

Neither speaks a word during the rest of their walk home. Sir Gordon is thinking of the past and building castles in the air for the future, and Stella Ray is telling herself again and again how beautiful was the face she had just seen, and trying

honestly to rejoice that her friend had
found the one piece of silver which alone
makes life perfect. Still, for the first
time, she is almost glad when they reach
home at last, and says good-bye more
hastily than is her wont, though she turns
and watches Gordon Leslie's tall slight
figure to the last, as he wends his way
slowly across the square, dreaming of all
the golden hours and sweet bright days
which have been conjured up before him
by a woman's smile.

CHAPTER X.

KINGSDENE.

" Here, where the world is quiet,
    Here, where all trouble seems
Dead winds' and spent waves' riot
    In doubtful dreams of dreams ;
I watch the green field growing
    For reaping folk and sowing,
For harvest-time and mowing,
    A sleepy world of streams."
                    Garden of Proserpine.

OWARDS the end of a long, hot September day, two ladies were sitting on the upper terrace at Kingsdene, engaged in the favourite occupation of drinking five o'clock tea. Mrs. Brabazon was dressed in crape from head to foot, and the widow's cap sitting somewhat awry on her head, announced to all observers that Mr. Brabazon had taken his departure to another and a better world.

Since then the aunt and niece had

lived almost entirely alone together, for Clara had taken advantage of the general soft-heartedness which a family loss is apt to bring in its train, to quietly marry her junior clerk in the Foreign Office, and it being too early days as yet for the shoe to pinch much, she was now as happy in her own way as most selfish people generally are.

Kingsdene was one of those large, rambling Elizabethan houses built of dark red sandstone (now grey with age) which, in spite of their size, always look comfortable, cheery, and homelike. Though not standing on a hill, its garden descended in two great old-fashioned terraces down to the edge of the small park which lay between the house and the great London road half a mile off, thereby giving it the effect from that side of standing higher than it really did.

These terraces were wide and long, and edged with old grey walls on which stood quaint stone sun-dials and old-fashioned urns, bearing the arms and devices of many an old race as nearly worn out as themselves.

At each end of the lower terrace stood two enormous yew-trees, as ancient as the most time-worn part of the mansion itself, and the peacock standing close by with his gorgeous tail spread out in the sunshine, seemed quite in keeping with the grandeur of days gone by that seemed to hang over the place.

The house itself, though large, possessed so many small bright rooms with oriel windows and deep wide fireplaces, that no one could have dreamed of ever feeling lonely, or cold, or cheerless in it. An immense hall, with flowers standing in every corner of it and great tropical leaves bowing their heads in welcome to all entering guests, led into the dining-room and the large drawing-room, which latter was furnished in the more modern style of white and gold, and yellow damask. But a door at the far-off end of the hall took one into a small low room looking on to the terrace, the sides of which were wainscoted oak from ceiling to floor, with a wide open fireplace that could accommodate half a dozen at least on the oaken settles within it. This was the special room of the young mistress of the mansion, where not only were kept her books, paintings, and private belongings, but where also was transacted all the business of the house, and the old steward interviewed each month; for since Stella Ray had come of age (at nineteen, according to her grandfather's will), she had proved herself an energetic and most worthy chatelaine of Kingsdene, doing her best to learn how to fulfil the duties allotted to her, and not to leave the trust which had been given into her hands in those of strangers.

Not but what her free, Bohemian nature rebelled somewhat against the cut-and-dry, business-like views of the old steward, and she was apt to astonish that mild functionary by some sudden reckless order which, though effectual in its conclusion, was far too hasty in its mode of arriving at the said conclusion to appear at all seemly to that quiet, steady-going old man. Still Stella had gained an immense popularity amongst those who were poor or dependent on her, for not only had she a kind word and a bright look for high and low, but when it was wanted, her quick keen energy and decision of character made her an invaluable friend in time of trouble, whilst her own early years of poverty helped her to read aright and judge fairly of the truth or untruth in all sorrows and complaints laid before her.

With all her true brave woman's heart, she had fought down the strength of her hopeless love for Gordon Leslie; and though he would always have a place in her life which no one else should ever take, the girl had too much pride and simple common sense not to see the folly of grieving over a misfortune for which no one but herself was to blame, and which hit hard herself alone.

So his memory was put away with sad and loving regret, until such time as she could bring herself to go back to the old calm friendly affection of days gone by. Until then she would bide her time patiently.

"Stella, my dear, there were some visitors came to call here to-day. Morland came and asked me if he should let them in, but I said I thought you were out, so we decided not to."

"Quite right, auntie ; though I'll admit that I was hiding behind the big Cape jessamine in the conservatory all the time."

" But why, my dear ? Who were the people ?"

" Oh, only that big noisy Mr. Brownover and his equally noisy wife, who live on the other side of Winncote. I don't like them."

" I don't think they're a bad sort of people," observed Mrs. Brabazon in her kind hearty voice. " They're a little loud and noisy certainly, but I think it's only their way, Stella; it's good-natured chaff generally, after all."

" Yes, but scattered crumbs of good-natured chaff can easily be rolled into a little hard ball of spite that could hit pretty severely," responded her niece dryly, whose confidence in her fellow-creatures was somewhat less than was that of her relative.

"Well, you know your own likings best," said the latter good-humouredly; "but it's dull work for a blithe little body like you to see no one but an old aunt from morning till night. I wonder whether Lord Cunninghame has come to Winncote yet;" and Mrs. Brabazon glances cautiously at Stella to see how the latter move will be taken by that young lady.

"I neither know nor care," she answered shortly.

"But he has been so kind in giving us opera-boxes and sending you flowers all last season, that it would seem a little rude were we to ignore him totally should he come down here, my dear."

"Time enough when he comes then, auntie," said Stella gaily. "Don't let us lose our tempers over him until it's necessary. Who is that riding up the drive now?" she added inquiringly, shading her eyes with one hand to get a better look at a spare bent figure on a stepping grey cob, which was slowly approaching the house.

" It's the very man we were speaking of," answered Mrs. Brabazon, with a guilty knowledge that in her pocket at that very minute lay a note from Lord Cunninghame declaring his intention of riding over to see the two ladies that same afternoon.

" Talk of the devil, ahem! Then you knew he was coming, aunt?" and Miss Ray turned quickly and gave a keen glance at her companion as she spoke.

" Well, I had an idea—I mean he said

—yes, I rather *did* think he'd come to-day, Stella," responded Mrs. Brabazon desperately, floundering between a desire to speak the truth, and a still stronger one to conceal it, lest her niece's insubordination on this subject should be openly manifested to the expected visitor.

But Stella said not a word, and remained sitting beside the tea-table with more resignation than could have been expected from her; only the quick curl of her lip, and the significant "devil's tattoo" beaten on the gravel by her small foot, boded ill for the success of Miss Ray's elderly admirer, who was shortly after ushered on to the terrace where the ladies were sitting.

Francis Verulam, Lord Cunninghame, was one of a class common enough in the

13—2

last generation, almost unknown in this. Polished and courteous in manner, quiet and cynical in speech, *grand seigneur* from the crown of his fine-shaped head to the sole of his aristocratic foot—yet few men were more hated by all classes than himself; for his imperious manner towards those beneath him had left him few friends to boast of there, whilst his keen perception of weakness in others and his sarcastic tongue made him equally feared and disliked by most of his own *confrères.*

To do the man justice he had one great and good point in his nature, for neither in his young days, when he had enjoyed the doubtful reputation of being the wildest man of a very wild time, nor in his older ones, when he was universally acknowledged to be in some ways the

wickedest, had the honour of the Veru-
lams' ancient house ever suffered in word
or deed at his hands. Conservative to
the backbone in all tenets, actions, and
thoughts, he was liberal in one principle
alone: that of regarding his neighbour's
possessions as his own, whether it were
the latter's house, horses, servants, or
wife; and being as yet unblest with that
latter and crowning anxiety to a man's
life, no house in return was more
thoroughly placed at the disposal of his
guests than was his family mansion of
Winncote and all contained therein.

His best friends averred that it would
be an utter impossibility to convey to
Lord Cunninghame's mind that there
had been known such phenomena as
women who were truly good, pure, and

religious; for he had bigoted ideas of his own on that subject, and seldom missed an opportunity when in men's society of avowing his decisive opinion : that he had never known but *one* good woman in the world, and she had been his own mother. (There were enemies of his who added : that in making the latter exception he was perhaps not wholly disinterested.)

In outward appearance Lord Cunninghame was tall and thin, of the type of countenance one associates with the patricians of old ; a man who in olden times would have gone to his death on the scaffold with a white rose on his breast and a smile on his pale refined face; and who would calmly have taken a pinch of snuff whilst looking on at the preparations for the death of his best friend, or for his own. His clear-cut mouth had always either a sneer on its thin, bloodless lips, or else a suave polished smile, which had as much warmth in it as the gleam of a northern light seen on a midsummer's eve in the far north; and in the studied deference of his manner to women, and the cynical courtesy of his speech to men, could be traced the precepts of those who had been the profoundest worshippers of Voltaire, Rochefoucauld, and that great list of brother cynics, who long ere this have solved the problems which even *their* learning and wisdom, and knowledge of human nature, were unable to fathom whilst here on earth.

Looking at him as he walked slowly across the terrace from the house, Lord Cunninghame looked every inch a gentleman *de l'ancien régime;* and yet it needed but a glance at the expression of his quiet sardonic face, to make one understand the bitter enmity that has so often ere now sprung up between high and low, plebeian and patrician, even to raising many an historical and sanguinary monument before our eyes, lest we should e'en go our way and forget the lessons taught us in times gone by.

" This is really good of you, Lord Cunninghame," bursts out Mrs. Brabazon with hurried warmth and outstretched hand, striving vainly to conceal and atone for her niece's calm curtness of manner towards the new addition to their society.

" Not at all, my dear madam. On the contrary, it is I who am heavily indebted to you. Instead of a solitary afternoon at Winncote, only enlivened by the complaint of some wretched beggar who professes to have his family roof-tree tumbling down on his head (I think my tenants take a special delight in annoying me by their sensitiveness on that score), I find myself in the society of two charming ladies, and sitting in a beautiful garden, which as yet has deferred clothing itself in those autumnal tints so much beloved by artists, but so little appreciated by those who, like myself, see enough of the ' sere and yellow leaf' in their own faces and hearts. What more can a man have left him to desire ?"

Miss Ray's lip curled more than ever, but she only commented on the first part of her visitor's speech :

" I have heard that the cottages round Winncote are some of them very bad."

" The people *say* so," answered Lord Cunninghame with a slight shrug of his high, narrow shoulders, as if to express his total disbelief in anything like truth being found amongst the lower orders.

" But couldn't you see for yourself, Lord Cunninghame ?" inquired Stella earnestly, to whose ears many reports had come of the dirt, sickness, and misery to be found amongst the badly-drained, ill-ventilated cottages on the large Winncote estate.

" My dear Miss Ray," (and Lord Cunninghame carefully removed a crumb of cake from the cuff of his black coat, after handing a small piece of the same to "Collie," who had deprecatingly laid one tan paw on his knee), "I too was unsophisticated and enthusiastic at your age, and full of plans for the remedying of all evils under the sun; but *à quoi bon* to try and raise up a class which by every law of nature is meant to remain in the ignorance that alone makes bliss. You could make the Ethiopian change his skin, and the leopard his spots, ere you could make the lower orders aught but *canaille.*"

Stella Ray did not answer, but looked gravely across the park and out towards the distant London road, a cloud of dust on which showed where the wagons were returning heavily laden from the harvest-fields, in charge of those who had borne the burden and heat of the day to gather bread for this man, and such as he, to eat.

"I don't understand enough about it all to argue with any one as clever as yourself, Lord Cunninghame," she said at last, "so let us come and take a turn in the rose-garden instead, if you won't have any more tea? I have found a bush of late roses there that is really a sight worth looking at."

And Stella led the way with a graciousness most unusual to her manner when conversing with that elderly nobleman.

Mrs. Brabazon found an unexpected errand to the drawing-room imperative; so the two paced slowly down the terrace, and turned into the sheltered, quaint old garden kept sacred to the queen of flowers alone, and where one or two standards of *Gloire de Dijon* and the later blooming roses still held their own against the damp, decaying autumn air.

CHAPTER XI.

NOT TO BE BOUGHT WITH GOLD.

" The burden of bright colours.   Thou shalt see
    Gold tarnished, and the grey above the green ;
And as the thing thou seest thy face shall be,
    And no more as the thing before time seen.
And thou shalt say of mercy ' It hath been,'
    And living, watch the old lips and loves expire,
And talking, tears shall take thy breath between :
    This is the end of every man's desire."

A Ballad of Burdens.

"WHAT a delightful old place this is !" observed Lord Cunning-hame, as they sauntered down the sunlit grassy paths intersecting the rose-garden. " One can easily imagine what a favourite trysting-place it must have been for the court ladies and their gallants in the good old days of Queen Bess, when, in *affaires de cœur* at least, it was every man for himself." And he laughed a low wicked laugh as he took a pinch of snuff.

This was a habit which Lord Cunninghame prided himself on retaining, though
it had long since died out even amongst
the men of his own generation. He
acknowledged its inconveniences, but
maintained that it was the only vice
which the lower orders had more or less
left to the higher ones, and could therefore never be too highly prized by the
latter.

"Yes, it is a dear old place," assented
Stella Ray, and her eyes brightened at the
praise of her dearly-loved home.

"But don't you ever feel dull here
living as quietly as you do, Miss
Ray?"

This independent, out-spoken young
heiress, who let him see so plainly that
she neither loved nor feared him, was

rather an enigma to Lord Cunninghame;
and though at first it had been the convenient dovetailing of the Kingsdene and
Winncote estates which had been the
attraction towards his offering up himself
and the far-famed Cunninghame diamonds
to the shrine of Miss Stella Ray, of late
a feeling of almost respect had grown up
in his heart for the girl who so steadily
declined any part or share in the matri-
monial advances which her relatives had
made towards him on her behalf. Still,
his firm belief that " every woman has her
price," and that a far lower one than the
Cunninghame diamonds, made him con-
fident of his success as a wooer; and
though he had ridden over to Kingsdene,
determined to try his fate this very day,
there was neither timidity nor anxiety

expressed on his clever, still face, as he vainly tried to read the expression on the grave honest one beside him.

"I don't know what it is to be dull," answered Stella, "there's so much to do in the country. Now in London I certainly was bored to death sometimes, I'll acknowledge."

"But you wouldn't have been had you tried it under a new phase. What woman was ever 'bored' in London if she had unlimited horses and carriages, dresses, diamonds, and opera-boxes?"

And again Lord Cunninghame laughed to himself as he remembered how many a once true heart had sold itself, and many a fair white soul had played its last stake, for the sake of even a few months' enjoyment of those glittering pleasures he spoke of.

"No, perhaps I should have liked it then," admitted Stella frankly.

The opportunity was not to be lost.

"Miss Ray, I came here to-day to speak to you on a subject of great importance to myself, though I scarcely dare think it may be of as much to you.   May I speak?"

The slight tremble in Lord Cunninghame's voice was a studied reflex of the tremor which had shaken his very heart and soul long time ago, as he pleaded for dear life with the one woman whose memory his many years of wasted love and life had been unable even yet utterly to drive from out his selfish heart—his one, first love! True, he had sacrificed *her* as easily as he had done all others, but her vengeance lay in his inability to forget her true good face, and sweet, loving words, and as long as life should last, no other woman's eyes would ever look so faithfully into his as did those of his old, dead love!

" Certainly, Lord Cunninghame."

The answer was courteous, but the tone scarcely encouraging.

" I came here to-day intent on discovering if those dreams of happiness which have of late seemed almost less visionary than usual, were in good truth likely at last to take a real shape and form; and whether in these, my later years at least, I should taste of the cup whose sweetness has so long been withheld from me—I mean that of home-happiness. I am a solitary man, Miss Ray, and years of loneliness, even more than age, have made me little fitted for the companionship of one so young and bright as yourself; but if you will marry me, I swear to Heaven you shall not repent it, and whatsoever man can do to give you happiness, that all shall be yours!"

" It cannot be, Lord Cunninghame. I am sorry, but I *could* not marry you."

For the first time in his life, did his own self-appreciation fail to blind Lord Cunninghame as to the decisive nature of this the only repulse he had ever known.

" You *cannot !* and why ?"

The suavity had left his voice, and a stern harsh tone had taken its place.

"Because I do not like you, Lord Cunninghame, and—will you be angry?"

"No; proceed!"

"And I wouldn't marry you even if my last hope of life depended on my doing so."

"Again may I ask why?"

"It's not because you're old," and the obnoxious adjective sounded almost sweet when said in those clear young pitying tones, "for I should not have minded that so very much, but every thought and feeling of yours and mine would be different, Lord Cunninghame, and how then could we know happiness? You hate the poor, I love them; you dislike a country life, I could not live without it; your pleasures are all great ones, mine so small that you could not even see any pleasure in them.   No, believe me, I am grateful to you " (a slight curl of the lip somewhat contradicted the speaker's words), " but were I to accept what you have offered me, I should be doing you a terrible injustice, and myself a wrong, which neither time nor years could efface."

Lord Cunninghame remained silent, as Stella's low, decisive tones rang out his rejection.   Not that he realised even yet that her answer was anything more than a woman's " nay," nor that her decision was meant as final; but the thought of defeat began to lend a new and strange value to victory, and for the first time he began to feel in earnest in his wooing.

" You are right, Miss Ray, and though I am the sufferer, I cannot say otherwise.

What right have I to dream that you, in the spring-time of youth, and happiness, and beauty, would marry one to whom these things sound but as a story from far-off years? Only I would have tried so hard to make you forget the disparity of years between us, if you had given me the trial. Won't you think it over *once* more before you give me your final decision? I know that at my age, and with my grey hairs " (to do his lordship justice, the latter, thanks to the exertions of Messrs. Truefitt, were almost invisible), " I am no fitting match for you, who are only in the dawn of your womanhood, but I have much to offer that could give a woman happiness, and no stone should be left unturned to gain it for you. Will you not give me the smallest hope ?"

" No, I cannot."

Lord Cunninghame smiled sarcastically, and continued :

" Then may I ask why you were good enough to receive me as courteously as you did to-day, and why you acceded so readily to my wish for conversation with your fair self, when you knew perfectly well what was the subject I wished to speak on ? Was it to encourage me in forgetting for the moment how many summers have passed over my head, or was it that you might have the pleasure of knowing you had contributed one more instance to fill the record of man's folly and woman's vanity, that you did this thing ?"

Stella's face flushed crimson at the taunt, and her eyes blazed as she drew herself up to her full height and faced her foe.

"You're wicked, *very* wicked to say such things, Lord Cunninghame, and were I a man, and you not an old one, I should like to punish you as you deserve."

His lordship smiled sardonically and took a pinch of snuff. A man who had been "out" with some of the most noted duellists of his day, could afford to despise all threats of imaginary vengeance.

"I was civil to you to-day because I wanted to get it over—that was all."

"Get *what* over, Miss Ray?" and the keen eyes quietly scrutinised her angry face.

"Why your — that is — I mean I thought you *did* mean to ask me to marry you," answered Stella, flushing hotter than ever but speaking out bravely, "and so I wanted to tell you at once that it was quite—quite impossible; to save you the trouble, you know."

"Very good of you, I must say; but you should have remembered that what is often done to others for their good, frequently ends by doing them a very great deal of harm. Forgive me if I have angered you, Miss Ray, and let us be friends. Remember, that in asking you to be my wife, I have but paid you the highest compliment that any man can pay any woman, and even now I can scarcely see why you should have rejected my offer so decisively."

"Because I cannot love you, and no woman should marry you without that," was the steady answer.

For once in his life does Lord Cunninghame feel that there *is* a power in human
hearts which is far greater than he had
dreamed of in his philosophy ; and a
strange yearning comes over his soul for
the days so long gone by, when he too
had had the power to make women's eyes
droop before the fire in his own, and pale
cheeks to flush at the passionate fervour
of words which then came from the heart
alone.

"Good-bye, Miss Ray," is all he says
simply ; but as Stella holds out her hand
quickly and looks him straight in the face
with her honest brown eyes, he adds
slowly : "And thank you for having
treated what was perhaps a more pre-
sumptuous offer than I thought, with the
kind good sense which at least leaves me

the power to call you 'friend,' if nothing
more."

And he turns and walks back to the
house, from whence in a few more minutes
the stepping grey cob carries him away as
sedately as before.

As he rides along on the way towards
his grand solitary home, the scene which
he has just passed through in the rose-
garden appears again and again before
him, for strange to say it was the first
time in his life that a woman had said
him nay; and yet, in spite of all, he
cannot but respect the outspoken girl
whose honesty of heart and purpose had
remained proof even against the glittering
temptation of the Cunninghame diamonds.
Still, he was sorry, for he felt lonely at
last; and even the renouncing of his

liberty would have been a small sacrifice
compared to the possession of a bright
young face that would lend radiance to his
life and home.

Was it fancy that brought before him
to-day of all others, the fair sweet face of
his dead love of old ? Even now he can
once more see the trusting look in her
deep blue eyes as they were raised to his
with the faith which even to the last
remained so firmly true. Never again,
Lord Cunninghame, will you see that
look in woman's eyes — never, never
again.

Meantime Stella had remained standing
in the rose-garden where he had left her.
Her cheeks burned still at the recollection
of the unpleasant ordeal she had just gone
through, and yet like a very woman, she

felt ready to excuse even a man as old as was her late suitor, for betraying the folly over which she might have reigned as queen ; and an unpleasant idea came home to her that she would find some difficulty in soothing Mrs. Brabazon's indignation over the treatment of that lady's pet *protégé*, Francis Lord Cunninghame.

A short bark of impatience from " Collie," who was anxiously awaiting a move on the part of his young mistress, aroused her to the fact that the sooner she broke the news to her expectant relative the better.

" Though we've done quite right, ' Collie,' my dog ! very, very right," she said confidentially to her canine friend, who wriggled his black-and-tan body into the most ghastly contortions, and grinned to show his fine teeth, and said more with his eyes and tail than many Christians could have done in words.

" Well ?" ejaculated her aunt, in a tone of breathless suspense, as Stella walked quietly into the drawing-room where that lady was making believe to be very busy sorting wools of the most impossible colours and shades.

" Well, aunt," answered her hardened niece, " why didn't you come out again just now ?"

" Because I thought my room was better than my company, just that, my dear !"

" Perhaps it was for once, auntie, for it gave me a chance of telling Lord Cunninghame my mind."

" My dear Stella, did he propose to

you ?" inquired Mrs. Brabazon breathlessly.

" Yes, I think so."

" *Think* so ! why you must know, child."

" Well, yes, he did, I suppose, though at one time I wasn't so sure that I hadn't declined the honour of his hand before it had ever been offered to me."

" Declined ? Then you've actually refused him ! Oh, Stella, Stella !" and tears of mortification fairly rolled down Mrs. Brabazon's cheeks.

" I'm afraid I did, auntie ; but you mustn't cry over spilt milk, you know."

" Yes, but the diamonds, and the two properties joining so nicely," moaned Mrs. Brabazon, utterly refusing to be comforted.

15—2

"And what good would they be to me if I married a man I hated, and were simply miserable?" inquired Stella calmly.

Mrs. Brabazon vouchsafed no reply beyond a feeble sob of intense disappointment at the failure of all her long-cherished hopes of seeing Stella become Lady Cunninghame. Still, finding herself no match for the latter's clear, plain arguments, and gradually thawing before the influence of the girl's gay, loving manner, she finally gave up the contest with a good grace, though ponderous sighs during all the rest of the evening testified mutely to the force of the disappointment which the events of that day had brought her.

CHAPTER XII.

A MERRY CHRISTMAS.

"Forget not yet the tried intent
    Of such a truth as I have meant,
    My great travail so gladly spent,
        Forget not yet !

"Forget not yet when first began
    The weary life ye know, since whan
    The suit, the service none tell can ;
        Forget not yet !

"Forget not then thine own approved,
    The which so long hath thee so loved,
    Whose steadfast faith yet never moved—
        Forget not this !"

SIR T. WYAT.

T is Christmas Eve, and in spite of a bitter east wind and an occasional fall of sleet and snow, there is brightness over all the land. Bright blaze the fires in the old mansion of Kingsdene, and brighter still look the faces of the church choir as they stand in the grand old hall that is hung round with holly and mistletoe, and sing their time-honoured hymns of praise for the " peace on earth and goodwill towards men " which the morrow will commemorate.

Bright too look the streets of our great metropolis to-night, and even a slight London fog can scarcely dim the clear starlight shining so pure and cold above the well-lit, busy streets. Crowds of women pass to and fro, laden with baskets containing good things for the Christmas dinner to-morrow, and each man as he meets his fellow nods a more cheery "good-night" than is his wont. The children (to whom alone "a merry Christmas" is a reality still and no vague memory only) are most of them asleep by now; the happy ones because they must needs wake next morning so *very* early (is it not Christmas Day to-morrow?), the desolate ones because, even to them, at night comes the one solace of their miserable lives: the waters of Lethe, a dreamless sleep.

Even the latest condemned prisoner, who only a month ago was a gay light-hearted village lad, whose hot blood was given as his excuse for words and blows too often meant in bitter earnest, and now lying on his straw bed in gaol under sentence of death for the murder of a comrade—even he is sleeping as peacefully as a little child on this, his last Christmas Eve. Who knows what dreams of the happy days of yore come before his mind? dreams in which the very lad who died by his hand so few short weeks ago, was still his brother and his friend. A smile as sweet as a woman's sweeps over his care-worn, sleeping face, and once more he hears his comrade's merry laugh as they strolled through the fields together last Christmas morning, and the awful scenes through which he has so lately passed fade away like a nightmare when day is dawning. Gone is the memory of the hot crowded court, the sarcasms of contending lawyers, the bitter angry faces of a mob crying out in a silence plainer than words, " Blood for blood," and the shamestricken, shrinking figure at the bar ; and vanished too are the cold clear tones of the judge as he pronounces the awful sentence, " to be hung by the neck until you are dead," and the falter that shakes his voice as he solemnly adds, " and may God have mercy upon your soul !"

But no brighter look is on any man's face to-night than on that of Sir Gordon Leslie, as he jumps out of his hansom at the door of Long's Hotel in Bond Street, about eleven p.m., on his return after an absence of many months ; and though the decisive negative given to the usual inquiry : " Any letters for me ?" brings a momentary frown upon it, all is speedily forgotten before the physical comforts of an excellent supper and a bottle of Clicquot's best, and still more in dreams of the great joy awaiting him to-morrow.

In one more hour will have dawned the day so anxiously hoped, so wearily waited for—when he can go to the woman whom he has loved so long and so faithfully, and ask for his reward at last.

What will she say ? How will she look ? " She *cannot* look anything else but beautiful, she *must* be all that is sweet and true," thinks the man who would count the world well lost for sake of her.

Since he had gone abroad, now many months ago, he had only written two or three times to Ida Villiers; in the first letter he had plainly intimated that out of respect for herself he should never seek to be more to her than the most ordinary friend, until such a time as he could come forward and try to win her as his wife in the face of the whole world.

The man's very refinement of nature made him heartily approve of the extreme frigidity of Ida's replies to him. Not for worlds would he have had his pure fair lily forget the honour due unto the man sleeping so calmly in his grave under the blue Italian skies; and day by day he raised his ideal higher, and worshipped before it with more and more infatuation of mind, as only strong reckless natures do who love for the first time, and almost invariably love without return.

He looks at his watch impatiently. It is only one o'clock, and more than twelve hours must elapse before common etiquette will allow him to go and see Mrs. Villiers. Still it is *the same day* now, any way, and the thought of that alone brings unspeakable happiness with it; and so Gordon Leslie's dreams, when he does at last betake himself to bed, are as radiant and joyous as any man's on this whole earth to-night.

Outside the wind still blows in cold and bitter blasts, and the snowflakes fall silently one by one in their stilly whiteness on the now deserted streets; but "peace on earth" already reigns over more than half the world, and "goodwill towards men" *must* come with the morning's sun.

*   *   *   *   *

It is the afternoon of Christmas Day, and two people are together in the quiet, prettily-furnished rooms in C—— Street, which Mrs. Villiers has made her home of late. The fire burns cheerily in the grate, and crackles out a " Merry Christmas" to the frosty sunbeam which is peeping in at the window and making odd lights and shadows to dance over the light blue walls and soft Cretonne chintzes all around. But it can give no brightness to the cold pale face of Ida Villiers as she stands confronting the stern, angry man, who strives to the very last in hoping against hope, for very love's sake.

" Ida, Ida, you cannot mean it ?"

"I do mean it, Sir Gordon," and the speaker's voice rings out pitilessly calm and clear.

"You wish me to believe that you were playing me false all along? That the woman I have so loved and worshipped was nothing more than an ordinary coquette, who leads men on until they would ruin body and soul for her, and then says : 'Go, I want you no more !' Ida, for your sake and mine, I dare not think it true."

"You may say what you please, or think what you like about me, Sir Gordon, but one fact remains : that I do not marry you!"

"Why not? For pity's sake, why not? Have I not been as true to you as mortal man can be, and did you not know that whilst you lived no other woman could ever come between us ?"

"Yes, I know," and in spite of herself Ida Villiers' voice falters, and a weak desire creeps into her heart to tell him how she too had often thought of his kind, handsome face, which never yet has looked coldly on her.

"Then why won't you care for me now as you did a year ago?" breaks out Sir Gordon passionately. "What is it, Ida, that comes between us?"

For an instant she hesitates. Is the future really worthy of the present sacrifice? she vaguely wonders. But it is too late to think of that now! And though her cheeks grow paler and paler, and her hands play nervously with her jewelled rings like one ill at ease, she speaks out his sentence and her own.

"What comes between us, you ask, Sir

Gordon ?" she says with a hard, low laugh. " Only this : that I am going to marry Lord Cunninghame within a month from now."

" Marry Lord Cunninghame !"

For a moment he cannot grasp her meaning fully; then it strikes home to his heart and mind in all its bitter force.

" Ida, my darling, I cannot believe it ! Have you so soon forgotten our happy days of long ago, when for the first time in my life I learnt to love as no man ever loves again ? Have you forgotten the long bright days, the sweet still evenings ? O God ! *can* you forget all ?" and the speaker's fair, handsome face is lined with agony.

" I have forgotten long since," answers Mrs. Villiers in a low, almost sullen voice.

"What pleasure will life bring to you if you marry such a man as that, Mrs. Villiers? 'Twere better far that you had to work for your daily bread, than sell all that is pure and good in you to live with a man whom you neither love nor respect!"

"I *have* worked for my daily bread, and for that very reason can judge for myself of what I am doing, better than even you can, Sir Gordon."

"But when there is no necessity for you to work, Ida? I am not a rich man, but I have enough money to give you all you could desire, darling. For God's sake don't throw me over for that! If you had learnt to care for any one who was a real good fellow—and I knew you could not help it, dear—Heaven knows I should have been the last to speak, for what am I that

I can dare reckon myself worthy of such as you? But that man, Lord Cunning-hame, you *cannot* care for, Mrs. Villiers, and you dare not look me in the face and tell the lie!"

"No," returns Ida wearily, "I do not 'care' for him, as you call it, at least not much; but I shall be very happy."

"Do you think you will? Do you think that you can sell your life, in all its youth and beauty, health and strength, to a bondage to which gold alone gives bright-ness? Did I believe you to be such a woman as that, I could but say, 'Thank God she is nought to me!' But I cannot, will not believe it. Are you trying me, Ida? Won't you even yet believe that you have been my first and only love, such as never man had? Dear one, ever since

16—2

I first saw you, all other women on earth have seemed to me but shadows that only come and go, and since I have known you, no other thought has ever filled my heart and mind but my thought of you, my darling, my own! Ida, Ida, you *shall* be mine! What right has any one on God's earth to come between us now?"

A half-doubting look crosses Mrs. Villiers' face. Was it really true, all this he said, or were they only the wild words of a man in the first flush of disappointment? If she did but know whether she had heart enough to be happy with *him*, and let the riches go for which she felt she was selling her woman's heart and soul! Would it be all in vain? Would they really prove only Dead Sea apples in the bitter end? And Ida's face looks sad and grave, as her good angel makes one more last effort to save her soul alive !

But the weight of the Cunninghame diamonds weighs down the scale heavier and heavier; so heavily, that neither a woman's bartered love nor a man's lost faith can for one instant hold their own against those glittering millstones; and when Ida Villiers lifts up her eyes and speaks, the die is cast for good · and all.

" It is no use your saying any more, Sir Gordon, for nothing can alter my determination now. It is best so, far best. Please go, for it is no use to prolong a conversation which only gives unhappiness to us both."

" *Unhappiness!* Is that the soft-sounding name you give to the torture which turns a man's heart into that of a fiend ? Will there never be any punishment on earth for those who play with the hearts and souls of others, until they have won from them all that makes life worth having, and then say, 'Go, forget ! I have had enough ' ? And yet even now I cannot wish to see you punished, my own, my darling ! No ; to the last I will only say 'Amen' to any sentence you may put upon me ; and if mine has been the sin in loving you too much, mine, too, at least will be the punishment. Good-bye, Ida ! Give me one kind hand-clasp before I go !" And the most loyal hand and heart that ever woman won, was laid at her feet that winter's day.

"Good-bye, Sir Gordon, and indeed I am sorry, more than you think, perhaps," falters Mrs. Villiers, with a miserable sense of having chosen the shadow for the substance, now that it is too late. And as Gordon Leslie turns and goes straight to the door without one backward look, her eyes follow his tall, fair-haired figure wistfully; and when the door closes behind him, Ida Villiers buries her face in her hands, and for the first time in her life weeps bitter, heartfelt, blinding tears, at the thought of the gallant, kindly face, with its frank, true smile, the life and light of which she has cut off from herself for evermore.

CHAPTER XIII.

A HAPPY NEW YEAR.

" 'What is life? what is death? what the false? what
        the true?
And what is the harm that one woman can do?'
Vain! all vain! . . . . For when, laughing, the wine
        I would quaff,
I remember'd too well all it cost me to laugh.
Through the revel it was but the old song I heard,
Through the crowd the old footsteps behind me they
        stirr'd,
In the night wind, the starlight, the murmurs of even,
In the ardours of earth, and the languors of heaven,
I could trace nothing more, nothing more through the
        spheres,
But the sound of old sobs, and the tracks of old
        tears!"

Lucile.

HE door of Mrs. Villiers' house shut to noisily and angrily, as if to speed the parting guest, whilst Sir Gordon Leslie walked slowly down C—— Street, like one in a dream. Was *this* the end to all his hopes and anticipations? Had those visions of happiness been but a mirage after all? Only a Fata Morgana luring him on to ruin, body and soul! He felt almost too bitterly hurt and angry to realise at first the heaviness of the blow which had fallen upon him, and a stunned feeling, such as he could only remember as yet to have felt after some severe physical shock, seemed numbing his faculties, and turning every thought in his brain to dire confusion.

He wandered on and on, from street to street, with the aimless and restless step of one who tries to tire out thought itself, though no one looking at his fair, frank face could have guessed at the misery hid under that quiet, calm exterior. Like all men of deep feeling and of sensitive nature, there was nothing Gordon Leslie hated so much as the wearing of a heart upon a sleeve, and to every passing acquaintance his recognition was as gay and his smile as cheery as of old ; but after a while, when by chance a semi-intoxicated cabman wished him ' A Merry Christmas,' a look of such

savage wrath blazed up in his eyes, as made
even the not very discerning Jehu observe to
his companion, *sotto voce :* " *That* swell ain't
'ad his fill o' good cheer to-day, poor chap !"

The memory of the next few days which
followed so slowly after each other, seemed
for months nothing but a long evil dream
to the man who had left all hope behind,
as surely as did they who entered the
portals of Dante's " Inferno." Each memory of bygone days, each ray of olden
brightness—the sound of a well-known bar
of music, or a woman's voice—had power
to turn the very light of the sun into
sudden darkness for him.

Though " only a year ago " is the
requiem sung over many a life's story, and
though to " remember " seems the one
thing harder even than to " forget," here

and there in the world are hearts and minds to whom the former is a hopeless reality, the latter a longed-for impossibility. Time may do wonders, years may deaden pain, but deep down in the truest hearts of all will lie the memory of those days of yore, when faith and truth were still bright living powers in our hearts and minds, not dim vague shadows only; and when the love now lying so peaceful and dead in its quiet grave, was the glorious reality of life's most radiant hours.

Where is now the pure faith, the unselfish devotion, so freely and so lovingly offered at the shrine of our sweet first love? Now we calculate on " gold" to be given for our " gold;" then we were content to take silver only in exchange for our richest, purest, golden treasure.

The first time one is "hard hit," one is ready and willing to do anything and everything that entails self-sacrifice ; somehow, then, the sun which is pouring down on our devoted heads scarce seems hot, because another likes to bask in it, and hours of waiting in a bitter east wind are well rewarded by a brief word or passing glance ; but later on one can think more calmly, and spare others as well as one's self much misery, by seeing in time that the sun *can* scorch and the wind bite hard : " Oh, le bon vieux temps quand j'étais si malheureux !"

The days dragged wearily on for Gordon Leslie, though in all outward seeming life seemed not one whit altered to him. The same faces met him at the covert-side, the same smiles welcomed him as of old, but the charm of life had gone never more to return. Sleepless hours, full of bitter thoughts and maddening memories, had not as yet shaken at least his nerve ; and when hounds were running hard over the strong vale country, no man could " hold his own," or cut out the work for others, more resolutely and quietly than did Sir Gordon Leslie.

More than one friend made the comment that " Leslie looked as if he'd had a facer," and more than one woman wondered why the smile whose power she had so often gauged ere this, seemed powerless to kindle an answering one in the grey eyes that now never lost their dreamy, absent look ; but not one amongst the many guessed the havoc which that " Merry Christmas " had wrought in the kindest, most loyal heart that ever man possessed. Verily, a saying only too often justified is this: "How to the word 'passion' the old Latin meaning clings—how truly it is a 'suffering'!"

There was but one human being in whose society Gordon Leslie could feel almost happy, and that was Stella Ray. The girl's gay nature and strong decision of character roused him sometimes in spite of himself, and brought him momentary forgetfulness, whilst her quiet, unobtrusive sympathy, felt, but never spoken, soothed him and gave him a feeling of rest which he could gain nowhere else. Slowly he learnt to read the true nature of her feelings for himself, his own pain making him quick to perceive and understand that of others, and a deep gratitude sprang up in his heart, such as can be felt by those alone who having been sorely wounded, receive an unexpected kindness which somewhat softens the bitterness of a disappointed life.

More than once did the idea of making Stella Ray his wife cross his mind, but the knowledge of how little he had to offer her —not even love itself—stood as an invincible barrier in his way.

People do not nowadays become melodramatic over their sorrows, and on the day that Ida Villiers was married, Sir Gordon Leslie neither tore his hair, nor raved, nor swooned, but simply went out hunting. Not even his horses found out that there was anything amiss with the master they carried that day, for he was not a man to wreak his vengeance and disappointment on anything of the brute creation. True, in discussing that day's sport over their claret at night, his friends casually observed that " Leslie went to hounds as if he kept a dozen spare necks in a drawer at home, judging by the amount of timber he rode a raw four-year-old at." And though the same intelligent observers give it as their opinion, "that a man can ride like that if he's never yet had a bad fall," on no one's mind did it dawn that there can be mental falls which madden for the minute and injure for ever after, far worse and more fatal in their effects than are any bodily ones. " People are *not* quite the same as they were before, after it; their few years of 'Sturm und Drang' are the heating in the furnace which qualifies the metal; their effect, however invisible, is never quite lost."

By the time that the sunny month of May came round, with its buds and flowers and its promises of summer, Sir Gordon Leslie had more or less made up his mind to forget the past, and live only for the present and future, and though the sense of pain which made itself felt in his heart at the mere mention of Ida Cunninghame's name, showed how hard a death his first love was dying, still to all intents and purposes he went about the world as gay and free from care as of old.

The London season was a late one this year, and even by the middle of May the scanty crowd in the Park and the streets gave one more the idea of early spring than summer, and the day of Stella Ray's presentation at her first Drawing-room was ushered in by showers of blinding sleet and a bitter east wind. Sir Gordon Leslie wended his way towards E——n Square, to call at Mrs. Brabazon's, just as most of the carriages containing fair freights, clad in satin, velvet, and lace, and surmounted by the orthodox tulle and feathers, were returning from Buckingham Palace; and he was so occupied in trying to find a dry spot at which to cross to the opposite side of the street, that a carriage passing him by closer than was pleasant on so muddy a day, decorated his irreproachable toilette with two or three large splashes.

He gave a look of annoyance at its disappearing wheels, but as neither the high-stepping black horses nor the gorgeous white and scarlet liveries of that vehicle were known to him by sight, he vouchsafed it no further attention.

Apparently, however, the occupant of the carriage in question knew Sir Gordon himself, for over her calm still face passed a look of surprise and almost of sorrow, and her proudly-carried head bent low, as if under some greater weight than that of the magnificent diamonds encircling it.

But he himself went on his way, unknowing and unconcerned, and was soon ushered into the big drawing-room at Mrs. Brabazon's house, where he found Stella Ray seated in state, and clad in plumes and train, having just been safely deposited at her aunt's door by the W——shire magnate, who had done the young heiress the honour of presenting her to her Sovereign.

Mrs. Brabazon and Lady Bland were the only other inmates of the room, and the latter struggled vainly to elicit from her cousin some account of the most striking toilettes which might that day have come under her observation.

"I don't believe any of the young girls can have looked better than yourself, my dear," said Mrs. Brabazon heartily. "Now doesn't she look nice, Gordon?"

Stella laughed out gaily, but blushed nevertheless as she caught Sir Gordon's critical and approving glance of admiration.

With her great dark eyes and red-bronze hair, shining out from clouds of soft white tulle and curling feathers, Stella Ray's face was one not easily to be overlooked; and though it was too dark and pale to look its best when clad in so trying a costume as "all white" by daylight, the glowing red lips lent a touch of colour, and the ever-changing expression a charm, which themselves alone were quite sufficient to excuse the length of gaze with which her criticiser favoured her.

" You wouldn't have thought much of me had you seen some of the other faces there, auntie, I can tell you," she said laughingly.

" Who was the best-dressed woman on the whole ?" inquired Lady Bland anxiously.

" Well, I can hardly say, Amelia. There was a black and yellow woman quite lovely, and then there was a pale blue woman I liked nearly as well. Oh yes, and a woman in black whom I liked almost best of all, I think."

" Can't you tell me more particulars

about their dresses than that?" asked Lady Bland discontentedly.

"I'll try and remember them by this evening, really, Amelia; but it can't amuse Gordon to listen to a talk of 'chiffons,' so let's defer it until then. I saw the most beautiful woman that I ever came across in my life to-day," added Stella, turning to Sir Gordon Leslie, "and that will interest you much more, won't it?"

"Of course," laughed he in answer.

"It was Lord Cunninghame's wife, who, as you know, was once Ida Stocker, the great actress and singer; and, oh! you can't think how perfectly lovely she is! As long as I live I shall never forget the impression she made upon me, as she swept past with her beautiful proud face, and her blaze of diamonds, which it fairly dazzled one's eyes to look at. And yet it wasn't a happy face quite, but somehow one forgot that in looking at her grand beauty and gorgeous diamonds."

The deep and exhaustive sigh which Mrs. Brabazon at this juncture thought it incumbent upon her to give, in memory of her niece's obstinate rejection of this same glittering coronet, attracted that young lady's mischievous attention entirely, and therefore the sudden start which Sir Gordon gave at the sound of his old love's name so carelessly spoken, passed unnoticed.

"Bear up, auntie," said Stella laughingly. "By the look of her ladyship's face she hasn't found the Cunninghame diamonds of sufficient value to outweigh the drawback of living perpetually in her husband's society. No, the more I looked at her face, the less I envied her. I cannot help thinking that I have seen her before somewhere, but I suppose not."

" Perhaps you've seen some photograph of her as an actress," observed Lady Bland spitefully. " Those sort of people always advertise themselves liberally."

Fortunately the fair Amelia did not catch the glance of indignant contempt which Sir Gordon's grey eyes flashed suddenly at her, but he only remarked calmly : " Perhaps ' those sort of people ' are more worthy of being objects of admiration than many of our other acquaintances."

" There's no accounting for tastes !" answered Lady Bland, shrugging her shoulders contemptuously, as she followed

Mrs. Brabazon out of the room ; " but it is quite beyond me to fathom why so singularly refined a man as Lord Cunninghame should have selected an ex-actress for his wife !"

END OF VOL. I.